FOR ETERNITY

(A Morgan Cross FBI Suspense Thriller—Book Nine)

BLAKE PIERCE

Blake Pierce

Blake Pierce is the USA Today bestselling author of the RILEY PAGE mystery series, which includes seventeen books. Blake Pierce is also the author of the MACKENZIE WHITE mystery series, comprising fourteen books; of the AVERY BLACK mystery series, comprising six books; of the KERI LOCKE mystery series, comprising five books; of the MAKING OF RILEY PAIGE mystery series, comprising six books; of the KATE WISE mystery series, comprising seven books; of the CHLOE FINE psychological suspense mystery, comprising six books; of the JESSIE HUNT psychological suspense thriller series, comprising thirty-five books (and counting); of the AU PAIR psychological suspense thriller series, comprising three books; of the ZOE PRIME mystery series, comprising six books; of the ADELE SHARP mystery series, comprising sixteen books, of the EUROPEAN VOYAGE cozy mystery series, comprising six books; of the LAURA FROST FBI suspense thriller, comprising eleven books; of the ELLA DARK FBI suspense thriller, comprising twenty-one books (and counting); of the A YEAR IN EUROPE cozy mystery series, comprising nine books, of the AVA GOLD mystery series, comprising six books; of the RACHEL GIFT mystery series, comprising fifteen books (and counting); of the VALERIE LAW mystery series, comprising nine books; of the PAIGE KING mystery series, comprising eight books; of the MAY MOORE mystery series, comprising eleven books; of the CORA SHIELDS mystery series, comprising eight books; of the NICKY LYONS mystery series, comprising eight books, of the CAMI LARK mystery series, comprising ten books; of the AMBER YOUNG mystery series, comprising seven books (and counting); of the DAISY FORTUNE mystery series, comprising five books; of the FIONA RED mystery series, comprising eleven books (and counting); of the FAITH BOLD mystery series, comprising fourteen books (and counting); of the JULIETTE HART mystery series, comprising five books (and counting); of the MORGAN CROSS mystery series, comprising ten books (and counting); of the FINN WRIGHT mystery series, comprising six books (and counting); of the new SHEILA STONE suspense thriller series, comprising five books (and counting); and of the new RACHEL BLACKWOOD suspense thriller series, comprising five books (and counting).

An avid reader and lifelong fan of the mystery and thriller genres, Blake loves to hear from you, so please feel free to visit www.blakepierceauthor.com to learn more and stay in touch.

ISBN: 978-1-0943-8461-0

BOOKS BY BLAKE PIERCE

RACHEL BLACKWOOD SUSPENSE THRILLER
NOT THIS WAY (Book #1)
NOT THIS TIME (Book #2)
NOT THIS CLOSE (Book #3)
NOT THIS ROAD (Book #4)
NOT THIS LATE (Book #5)

SHEILA STONE SUSPENSE THRILLER
SILENT GIRL (Book #1)
SILENT TRAIL (Book #2)
SILENT NIGHT (Book #3)
SILENT HOUSE (Book #4)
SILENT SCREAM (Book #5)

FINN WRIGHT MYSTERY SERIES
WHEN YOU'RE MINE (Book #1)
WHEN YOU'RE SAFE (Book #2)
WHEN YOU'RE CLOSE (Book #3)
WHEN YOU'RE SLEEPING (Book #4)
WHEN YOU'RE SANE (Book #5)
WHEN YOU'RE SILENT (Book #6)

MORGAN CROSS MYSTERY SERIES
FOR YOU (Book #1)
FOR RAGE (Book #2)
FOR LUST (Book #3)
FOR WRATH (Book #4)
FOREVER (Book #5)
FOR US (Book #6)
FOR NOW (Book #7)
FOR ONCE (Book #8)
FOR ETERNITY (Book #9)
FORLORN (Book #10)

JULIETTE HART MYSTERY SERIES

NOTHING TO FEAR (Book #1)
NOTHING THERE (Book #2)
NOTHING WATCHING (Book #3)
NOTHING HIDING (Book #4)
NOTHING LEFT (Book #5)

FAITH BOLD MYSTERY SERIES
SO LONG (Book #1)
SO COLD (Book #2)
SO SCARED (Book #3)
SO NORMAL (Book #4)
SO FAR GONE (Book #5)
SO LOST (Book #6)
SO ALONE (Book #7)
SO FORGOTTEN (Book #8)
SO INSANE (Book #9)
SO SMITTEN (Book #10)
SO SIMPLE (Book #11)
SO BROKEN (Book #12)
SO CRUEL (Book #13)
SO HAUNTED (Book #14)

FIONA RED MYSTERY SERIES
LET HER GO (Book #1)
LET HER BE (Book #2)
LET HER HOPE (Book #3)
LET HER WISH (Book #4)
LET HER LIVE (Book #5)
LET HER RUN (Book #6)
LET HER HIDE (Book #7)
LET HER BELIEVE (Book #8)
LET HER FORGET (Book #9)
LET HER TRY (Book #10)
LET HER PLAY (Book #11)

DAISY FORTUNE MYSTERY SERIES
NEED YOU (Book #1)
CLAIM YOU (Book #2)
CRAVE YOU (Book #3)
CHOOSE YOU (Book #4)
CHASE YOU (Book #5)

AMBER YOUNG MYSTERY SERIES
ABSENT PITY (Book #1)
ABSENT REMORSE (Book #2)
ABSENT FEELING (Book #3)
ABSENT MERCY (Book #4)
ABSENT REASON (Book #5)
ABSENT SANITY (Book #6)
ABSENT LIFE (Book #7)

CAMI LARK MYSTERY SERIES
JUST ME (Book #1)
JUST OUTSIDE (Book #2)
JUST RIGHT (Book #3)
JUST FORGET (Book #4)
JUST ONCE (Book #5)
JUST HIDE (Book #6)
JUST NOW (Book #7)
JUST HOPE (Book #8)
JUST LEAVE (Book #9)
JUST TONIGHT (Book #10)

NICKY LYONS MYSTERY SERIES
ALL MINE (Book #1)
ALL HIS (Book #2)
ALL HE SEES (Book #3)
ALL ALONE (Book #4)
ALL FOR ONE (Book #5)
ALL HE TAKES (Book #6)
ALL FOR ME (Book #7)
ALL IN (Book #8)

CORA SHIELDS MYSTERY SERIES
UNDONE (Book #1)
UNWANTED (Book #2)
UNHINGED (Book #3)
UNSAID (Book #4)
UNGLUED (Book #5)
UNSTABLE (Book #6)
UNKNOWN (Book #7)
UNAWARE (Book #8)

MAY MOORE SUSPENSE THRILLER
NEVER RUN (Book #1)
NEVER TELL (Book #2)
NEVER LIVE (Book #3)
NEVER HIDE (Book #4)
NEVER FORGIVE (Book #5)
NEVER AGAIN (Book #6)
NEVER LOOK BACK (Book #7)
NEVER FORGET (Book #8)
NEVER LET GO (Book #9)
NEVER PRETEND (Book #10)
NEVER HESITATE (Book #11)

PAIGE KING MYSTERY SERIES
THE GIRL HE PINED (Book #1)
THE GIRL HE CHOSE (Book #2)
THE GIRL HE TOOK (Book #3)
THE GIRL HE WISHED (Book #4)
THE GIRL HE CROWNED (Book #5)
THE GIRL HE WATCHED (Book #6)
THE GIRL HE WANTED (Book #7)
THE GIRL HE CLAIMED (Book #8)

VALERIE LAW MYSTERY SERIES
NO MERCY (Book #1)
NO PITY (Book #2)
NO FEAR (Book #3)
NO SLEEP (Book #4)
NO QUARTER (Book #5)
NO CHANCE (Book #6)
NO REFUGE (Book #7)
NO GRACE (Book #8)
NO ESCAPE (Book #9)

RACHEL GIFT MYSTERY SERIES
HER LAST WISH (Book #1)
HER LAST CHANCE (Book #2)
HER LAST HOPE (Book #3)
HER LAST FEAR (Book #4)
HER LAST CHOICE (Book #5)

HER LAST BREATH (Book #6)
HER LAST MISTAKE (Book #7)
HER LAST DESIRE (Book #8)
HER LAST REGRET (Book #9)
HER LAST HOUR (Book #10)
HER LAST SHOT (Book #11)
HER LAST PRAYER (Book #12)
HER LAST LIE (Book #13)
HER LAST WHISPER (Book #14)
HER LAST SECRET (Book #15)

AVA GOLD MYSTERY SERIES
CITY OF PREY (Book #1)
CITY OF FEAR (Book #2)
CITY OF BONES (Book #3)
CITY OF GHOSTS (Book #4)
CITY OF DEATH (Book #5)
CITY OF VICE (Book #6)

A YEAR IN EUROPE
A MURDER IN PARIS (Book #1)
DEATH IN FLORENCE (Book #2)
VENGEANCE IN VIENNA (Book #3)
A FATALITY IN SPAIN (Book #4)

ELLA DARK FBI SUSPENSE THRILLER
GIRL, ALONE (Book #1)
GIRL, TAKEN (Book #2)
GIRL, HUNTED (Book #3)
GIRL, SILENCED (Book #4)
GIRL, VANISHED (Book 5)
GIRL ERASED (Book #6)
GIRL, FORSAKEN (Book #7)
GIRL, TRAPPED (Book #8)
GIRL, EXPENDABLE (Book #9)
GIRL, ESCAPED (Book #10)
GIRL, HIS (Book #11)
GIRL, LURED (Book #12)
GIRL, MISSING (Book #13)
GIRL, UNKNOWN (Book #14)
GIRL, DECEIVED (Book #15)

GIRL, FORLORN (Book #16)
GIRL, REMADE (Book #17)
GIRL, BETRAYED (Book #18)
GIRL, BOUND (Book #19)
GIRL, REFORMED (Book #20)
GIRL, REBORN (Book #21)

LAURA FROST FBI SUSPENSE THRILLER
ALREADY GONE (Book #1)
ALREADY SEEN (Book #2)
ALREADY TRAPPED (Book #3)
ALREADY MISSING (Book #4)
ALREADY DEAD (Book #5)
ALREADY TAKEN (Book #6)
ALREADY CHOSEN (Book #7)
ALREADY LOST (Book #8)
ALREADY HIS (Book #9)
ALREADY LURED (Book #10)
ALREADY COLD (Book #11)

EUROPEAN VOYAGE COZY MYSTERY SERIES
MURDER (AND BAKLAVA) (Book #1)
DEATH (AND APPLE STRUDEL) (Book #2)
CRIME (AND LAGER) (Book #3)
MISFORTUNE (AND GOUDA) (Book #4)
CALAMITY (AND A DANISH) (Book #5)
MAYHEM (AND HERRING) (Book #6)

ADELE SHARP MYSTERY SERIES
LEFT TO DIE (Book #1)
LEFT TO RUN (Book #2)
LEFT TO HIDE (Book #3)
LEFT TO KILL (Book #4)
LEFT TO MURDER (Book #5)
LEFT TO ENVY (Book #6)
LEFT TO LAPSE (Book #7)
LEFT TO VANISH (Book #8)
LEFT TO HUNT (Book #9)
LEFT TO FEAR (Book #10)
LEFT TO PREY (Book #11)
LEFT TO LURE (Book #12)

LEFT TO CRAVE (Book #13)
LEFT TO LOATHE (Book #14)
LEFT TO HARM (Book #15)
LEFT TO RUIN (Book #16)

THE AU PAIR SERIES
ALMOST GONE (Book#1)
ALMOST LOST (Book #2)
ALMOST DEAD (Book #3)

ZOE PRIME MYSTERY SERIES
FACE OF DEATH (Book#1)
FACE OF MURDER (Book #2)
FACE OF FEAR (Book #3)
FACE OF MADNESS (Book #4)
FACE OF FURY (Book #5)
FACE OF DARKNESS (Book #6)

A JESSIE HUNT PSYCHOLOGICAL SUSPENSE SERIES
THE PERFECT WIFE (Book #1)
THE PERFECT BLOCK (Book #2)
THE PERFECT HOUSE (Book #3)
THE PERFECT SMILE (Book #4)
THE PERFECT LIE (Book #5)
THE PERFECT LOOK (Book #6)
THE PERFECT AFFAIR (Book #7)
THE PERFECT ALIBI (Book #8)
THE PERFECT NEIGHBOR (Book #9)
THE PERFECT DISGUISE (Book #10)
THE PERFECT SECRET (Book #11)
THE PERFECT FAÇADE (Book #12)
THE PERFECT IMPRESSION (Book #13)
THE PERFECT DECEIT (Book #14)
THE PERFECT MISTRESS (Book #15)
THE PERFECT IMAGE (Book #16)
THE PERFECT VEIL (Book #17)
THE PERFECT INDISCRETION (Book #18)
THE PERFECT RUMOR (Book #19)
THE PERFECT COUPLE (Book #20)
THE PERFECT MURDER (Book #21)
THE PERFECT HUSBAND (Book #22)

THE PERFECT SCANDAL (Book #23)
THE PERFECT MASK (Book #24)
THE PERFECT RUSE (Book #25)
THE PERFECT VENEER (Book #26)
THE PERFECT PEOPLE (Book #27)
THE PERFECT WITNESS (Book #28)
THE PERFECT APPEARANCE (Book #29)
THE PERFECT TRAP (Book #30)
THE PERFECT EXPRESSION (Book #31)
THE PERFECT ACCOMPLICE (Book #32)
THE PERFECT SHOW (Book #33)
THE PERFECT POISE (Book #34)
THE PERFECT CROWD (Book #35)

CHLOE FINE PSYCHOLOGICAL SUSPENSE SERIES
NEXT DOOR (Book #1)
A NEIGHBOR'S LIE (Book #2)
CUL DE SAC (Book #3)
SILENT NEIGHBOR (Book #4)
HOMECOMING (Book #5)
TINTED WINDOWS (Book #6)

KATE WISE MYSTERY SERIES
IF SHE KNEW (Book #1)
IF SHE SAW (Book #2)
IF SHE RAN (Book #3)
IF SHE HID (Book #4)
IF SHE FLED (Book #5)
IF SHE FEARED (Book #6)
IF SHE HEARD (Book #7)

THE MAKING OF RILEY PAIGE SERIES
WATCHING (Book #1)
WAITING (Book #2)
LURING (Book #3)
TAKING (Book #4)
STALKING (Book #5)
KILLING (Book #6)

RILEY PAIGE MYSTERY SERIES
ONCE GONE (Book #1)

ONCE TAKEN (Book #2)
ONCE CRAVED (Book #3)
ONCE LURED (Book #4)
ONCE HUNTED (Book #5)
ONCE PINED (Book #6)
ONCE FORSAKEN (Book #7)
ONCE COLD (Book #8)
ONCE STALKED (Book #9)
ONCE LOST (Book #10)
ONCE BURIED (Book #11)
ONCE BOUND (Book #12)
ONCE TRAPPED (Book #13)
ONCE DORMANT (Book #14)
ONCE SHUNNED (Book #15)
ONCE MISSED (Book #16)
ONCE CHOSEN (Book #17)

MACKENZIE WHITE MYSTERY SERIES
BEFORE HE KILLS (Book #1)
BEFORE HE SEES (Book #2)
BEFORE HE COVETS (Book #3)
BEFORE HE TAKES (Book #4)
BEFORE HE NEEDS (Book #5)
BEFORE HE FEELS (Book #6)
BEFORE HE SINS (Book #7)
BEFORE HE HUNTS (Book #8)
BEFORE HE PREYS (Book #9)
BEFORE HE LONGS (Book #10)
BEFORE HE LAPSES (Book #11)
BEFORE HE ENVIES (Book #12)
BEFORE HE STALKS (Book #13)
BEFORE HE HARMS (Book #14)

AVERY BLACK MYSTERY SERIES
CAUSE TO KILL (Book #1)
CAUSE TO RUN (Book #2)
CAUSE TO HIDE (Book #3)
CAUSE TO FEAR (Book #4)
CAUSE TO SAVE (Book #5)
CAUSE TO DREAD (Book #6)

KERI LOCKE MYSTERY SERIES

PROLOGUE

The sound of laughter and clinking glasses filled Sarah's new home as she stood in the doorway, welcoming her guests with open arms. Her eyes sparkled with elation as friends and family strolled into her living room, admiring the freshly painted walls and the carefully chosen decor. The housewarming party was in full swing, a lively celebration of her recent move.

"Sarah, you've really outdone yourself!" her cousin Emily gushed, taking in the spread of appetizers and wine bottles on the kitchen counter. "This place is lovely."

"Thank you," Sarah replied, beaming. "I feel lucky to have found it, especially after getting that job offer so last-minute."

"Speaking of which, how's your new position going?" Emily asked, sipping from her wine glass.

"Everything's been great so far. My coworkers are nice, and I'm slowly getting the hang of things," Sarah said, trying to sound confident. In truth, the move for this new job opportunity had been daunting, but Sarah wore her smile like armor, determined not to let her anxiety show.

Throughout the evening, she flitted from one group of guests to another, engaging in conversations about her new life, her job, and her beautiful home. She felt grateful for their support and encouragement, but beneath the surface, a quiet unease lurked. Change had never come easy to Sarah, and even though she put up a brave front, the enormity of her new beginning weighed heavily on her.

As the night began to wind down, guests lingered near the door, exchanging goodbyes and final well-wishes. Sarah hugged each one tightly, thanking them for coming and assuring them they were welcome any time. As the last guest stepped out into the cool night air, Sarah closed the door behind them with a soft click, feeling both relieved and proud. She had pulled off a successful party in her new home, and maybe, just maybe, change wasn't always a bad thing.

Sarah rolled up her sleeves and began to tidy the living room, gathering half-empty wine glasses and crumpled napkins. Her movements were methodical, each placement of a glass or toss of a napkin into the trash accompanied by a silent reminder that she had faced change before, and she could do it again.

"Nothing ventured, nothing gained," she murmured under her breath as she straightened a stack of coasters on the coffee table. Her eyes fell upon an unattended tall can of beer, which immediately struck her as odd. Everyone had been drinking wine tonight, and her friends weren't typically beer drinkers.

Did someone bring this in? she asked herself, picking up the can and examining it. The chill of the aluminum against her fingertips was strangely comforting. It's fine, she thought, placing it on the counter. Just a bit peculiar.

Suddenly, a gentle breeze brushed against her skin, causing her to shiver involuntarily. Sarah glanced around the room, searching for the source. Someone must have cracked a window.

Must've been Andrea, she thought, recalling how her friend was always warm. *Or maybe Greg, he likes some fresh air when he drinks.* As she approached the window, she couldn't help but feel a twinge of unease. She reached out to close it, but just as her hand touched the cold latch, a faint creak echoed from within another room.

"Hello?" Her voice trembled slightly. "Is someone still here?"

No response. She told herself it was probably just the house settling, but her heart raced in her chest regardless. Gathering her courage, she closed the window with a decisive click and took a deep breath. "Get a grip, Sarah," she whispered, attempting to quell her nerves. "It's just a noise. You've got this." And with renewed determination, she continued her cleanup, though her eyes couldn't help but dart around the room every so often, seeking out any sign of something amiss.

Sarah's unease grew stronger as she moved through the house—she could still feel a slight draft, like another window was open. She checked the locks on both the front and back doors. Her hands trembled slightly as she found each door still securely locked.

She checked the windows again. With every window she secured, Sarah's anxiety deepened, like an itch she couldn't quite reach. When she reached the last window, she noticed a chilling breeze coming from it, even though it appeared to be closed tight. She checked it again, only to realize the small window was slightly ajar. This was it—the culprit of the breeze.

Sarah barely had time to react before she felt a crushing blow to her head, a flash of white-hot pain searing through her skull. The world around her began to blur and spin, her vision narrowing into a tunnel of darkness. She could feel her body crumpling to the ground, every nerve screaming in agony as she fought to remain conscious.

But the darkness swallowed her whole, leaving only silence in its wake.

She turned her head slightly, trying to catch a glimpse of whatever—whoever—had done this. But all she could make out was the shape of a man's feet standing in front of her before another crushing blow rendered her plummeting into darkness.

CHAPTER ONE

The rhythmic thud of fists against a training dummy echoed through the dimly lit room. Sweat dripped from Morgan Cross's brow, dark strands of hair clinging to her face as she pummeled the lifeless figure with fierce determination. Each powerful punch and kick served as a reminder of her own strength, a defiance to the ghosts of her past that threatened to drag her down.

"Damn, I've still got it," she muttered under her breath.

At forty years old, Morgan knew she wasn't as spry as she used to be. But ten years in prison could do wonders for one's physical prowess. With nothing but time on her hands behind bars, she'd honed her body into a weapon, preparing for the day when she could finally clear her name and get her life back.

Pausing mid-punch, Morgan stepped back to catch her breath. She wiped her sweat-slicked face with a towel and took a swig from her water bottle. As the cool liquid slid down her throat, memories of her time in prison began to surface.

She wanted to move on. But it was easier said than done. The sting of betrayal festered within her, a wound that refused to close. Someone in the FBI had framed her for a crime she didn't commit. And though that person remained unknown, she did know someone else who was actively messing with her life: Agent Thomas Grady.

"Thomas," she hissed, clenching her fists at the thought of him. The handsome agent had wormed his way into her life, feigning friendship and even attempting romance. Yet all along, he'd been double-crossing her, working for the same men who'd sent her to prison.

And now, to make matters worse, he'd kidnapped her beloved dog, Skunk.

Morgan stepped out of the training facility into the warm nighttime air. The scent of freshly cut grass and the distant hum of traffic filled her senses as she walked across the parking lot towards her car. The weight of loneliness pressed down on her chest as she thought about returning to her empty house, where Skunk's presence was sorely missed.

"Damn it, Thomas," she muttered under her breath, clenching her fists at the memory of finding Skunk's collar on her coffee table. Alongside it, an ominous note from Thomas had sent shivers down her spine. He'd been making her play his twisted game before, but days had passed without a word from him. In the pit of her stomach, she couldn't help but fear the worst: that Skunk was gone for good.

But Thomas had to be bluffing. He had to be. There was no way…

Morgan focused on the road ahead, driving through the familiar streets of Dallas. Her fingers drummed impatiently on the steering wheel, her mind racing with possible scenarios and outcomes.

The moon cast a silvery glow on the quiet suburban street as Morgan's car rolled to a stop in front of her house. She squinted through the darkness, noticing another vehicle parked out front. The sleek black sedan was unmistakable – it belonged to Derik.

The last thing she wanted was company, especially when her thoughts were consumed by Skunk and Thomas's twisted game.

As soon as she pulled into the driveway, Derik stepped out of his car and jogged over to her. His green eyes seemed to glimmer in the moonlight, reflecting a mix of concern and determination.

"Hey, what are you doing here?" Morgan asked, trying to keep her voice level as she stepped out of her car. "Do you have any news about Thomas?"

Derik shook his head, his slick black hair glinting in the faint light. "No, I don't. I just... I didn't want you to be alone tonight."

Morgan scoffed, the memory of Derik's betrayal still fresh in her mind despite their slowly mending relationship. "I can handle myself, Derik. Go home."

She turned on her heel and marched toward her front door, but Derik followed closely behind. "Morgan, please. Let me help."

Morgan sighed, running her fingers through her dark hair. She knew Derik had been working tirelessly to make up for his past mistakes, and his concern was sincere. She had even confided in him about Thomas kidnapping Skunk, a secret she shared with no one else.

"Alright," she finally said, her voice wavering with vulnerability. "Come in."

They went into the house together, finding their spot on her living room couch, as they'd done so many times before. In the dimly lit living room, Morgan's tattoos seemed to dance on her skin. Derik cleared his throat, breaking the heavy silence that had settled between them.

"Look, Morgan," he began hesitantly, "it's not too late to bring the FBI and authorities in on this thing with Thomas."

Morgan's eyes flashed with anger, and she clenched her fists. "No, Derik!" she spat. "Thomas was very clear that he would kill Skunk if I tried to involve others. Maybe he already did... but if there's even a chance my dog is still alive, I have to wait for his instructions. I have to play his game, as much as I despise it."

Derik rubbed the back of his neck, frustration etched on his face. "I just don't like that we're not doing this by the book, Morgan. It doesn't feel right."

Morgan glared at him, her heart pounding in her chest. "Well, sometimes life doesn't go 'by the book,' Derik. Look at what happened to me! Ten years in prison for a crime I didn't commit! I trusted you to follow through with my wishes, and now you're questioning that?"

"Alright, alright," Derik conceded, raising his hands defensively. "I'll keep this between us. But just know that I've been trying to locate Thomas with my own resources, and so far, I haven't found anything."

Morgan's gaze softened, and she exhaled slowly. She knew Derik was putting himself on the line for her, and despite their rocky history, it meant something. "Thank you, Derik," she murmured, her voice low and sincere.

"Of course," he replied, his green eyes meeting hers with determination. "Whatever it takes, Morgan. We'll find Skunk and put an end to Thomas's games."

Glancing at the clock, Morgan realized how late it was. She stifled a yawn and rubbed her tired eyes. "I should try to get some sleep," she murmured.

"Wait," Derik said, his brow furrowing with concern. "You shouldn't be alone right now. What if Thomas has something worse planned for you? I don't like the idea of you staying here by yourself."

Morgan studied him for a moment, taking in his tired green eyes and the dark circles beneath them. She knew he meant well, but she didn't have the energy to argue with him. "Fine," she sighed, relenting. "You can crash on the couch."

"Thank you," he replied, relief washing over his face. "I just want you to be safe, Morgan."

"Goodnight, Derik," she said, her voice softening as she gave him a small, grateful smile before heading towards her bedroom.

"Night, Morgan," he called after her.

***

The forest swallowed Morgan whole, the darkness pressing in around her as she ran, her breath coming in ragged gasps. The moon struggled to illuminate her path, its light barely reaching through the thick canopy of leaves above. Her heart hammered in her chest, but she couldn't stop, not when her father's cabin was so close.

The familiar outline of the cabin loomed ahead, a beacon of safety in the night. But no matter how hard she pushed herself, it never seemed to get any closer.

"Come on," she muttered under her breath, desperation clawing at her throat. She needed to reach that cabin, needed to find refuge from whatever chased her through the forest.

As she stumbled over a tree root, her muscles screamed in protest, but she gritted her teeth and continued, determined to make it to the cabin.

The cabin loomed before her, but never within her grasp, leaving her stranded in a terrifying limbo.

Suddenly, the eerie silence of the forest was shattered by a chorus of barking. Morgan's heart leaped into her throat as she recognized the familiar sound of Skunk's voice. Desperation fueled her, and she sprinted faster, branches whipping at her face as she plunged deeper into the woods.

"Skunk!" she cried out, her voice raw and desperate as she called for her loyal companion. Sweat poured down her face, her muscles trembling from the relentless exertion. She needed to find him; there was no time to lose.

Finally, the cabin emerged from the shadows, its weathered wood and stone structure offering solace amidst the inky darkness. But her relief was short-lived when she spotted the figure standing on the porch. Thomas leaned against one of the wooden support beams, his handsome features twisted into a wicked grin as he held an old hunting rifle to Skunk's head.

"Thomas, you bastard," Morgan snarled, her eyes flashing with fury. "Let him go!"

"Ah, Morgan," Thomas taunted, his voice dripping with cruelty. "You finally made it. I was beginning to think you didn't care about your precious dog."

"Please, don't do this," she begged, her voice cracking with emotion. "He's innocent. This is between you and me."

"Is it, though?" he mused, his thumb brushing the trigger of the rifle. "Or is this just another piece in the game we've been playing?"

Morgan's heart raced, her thoughts whirling in panic. She had to find a way to save Skunk, but how? She tried to suppress the memories of her time behind bars, of the betrayal that led her there, and the darkness that threatened to consume her once more.

"Last chance, Morgan," Thomas sneered, tightening his grip on the rifle. "Are you willing to play by my rules?"

"Please," she whispered, tears streaming down her face as she locked eyes with Skunk. "Just let him go."

Thomas's smile widened, and his finger tightened on the trigger. A deafening bang echoed through the forest, and Morgan jolted awake, gasping for air. She sat up in bed, her sheets soaked in sweat, and the morning light filtering through her curtains.

Another nightmare.

She blinked away the tears that threatened to spill over, her heart still pounding in her chest. This one had been even more visceral than some of the others. As reality poured back in, she realized there was a banging coming from her door.

Right. Derik had stayed the night.

"Come in," Morgan called out, her voice strained as the banging continued. The bedroom door swung open, revealing a disheveled Derik, urgency etched on his face.

"Mueller wants us at HQ ASAP. We've got a case," he announced, before he took in Morgan's appearance, concern all over his face. "Morgan, are you okay?"

"I'm fine," she dismissed with a wave, pulling herself out of bed. "Let's just get to HQ."

"Are you sure? I—"

"I'm fine, Derik," she snapped, standing. Her legs felt weak, still trembling from the nightmare that had shaken her to the core. But though her trust in Derik was returning, she wasn't ready to confide in him, not yet.

He kept his distance and nodded, ducking out of the room. With that, Morgan got dressed. If they had another case, that could only mean another killer was on the loose.

CHAPTER TWO

The familiar sight of Assistant Director Mueller's office greeted Morgan and Derik as they stepped inside, the imposing figure of Mueller himself sitting behind his desk, waiting for them. Morgan's stomach twisted into knots; she'd never had a good relationship with the man, his mistrust of her palpable even now.

Morgan studied Mueller's face, the deep lines etched into his forehead betraying the seriousness of the matter at hand. She shifted her gaze to the neatly stacked pile of files on his desk, her instincts tingling with anticipation.

"Sit down," Mueller commanded, his voice firm and authoritative.

Morgan and Derik complied, settling into the rigid chairs before them. Morgan could feel the cold, hard metal pressing against her back, a reminder of the steel bars that had once defined her existence.

"A woman has been found dead in a small town just outside of the city," Mueller began, picking up one of the files from his desk. "Sarah Benson. She was found dead in her new home in Charlesberg after a housewarming party. No sign of forced entry."

Morgan leaned forward, resting her tattooed arms on her knees, her dark eyes narrowing as she processed the information. "So, it's obvious then – one of the people at the party killed her."

Mueller shook his head, his expression unyielding. "At first glance, it might look like that. But there's a reason why the case was brought to the FBI. We believe Sarah isn't the first victim."

A spark of anger ignited within Morgan, fueling her determination to find justice for those who had been wronged. She clenched her fists, feeling the familiar weight of responsibility settle upon her shoulders. Memories of her own wrongful imprisonment lingered in the shadows of her mind, propelling her to fight even harder for the truth.

"Wait," Derik interjected, his green eyes narrowing with suspicion. "What do you mean she's not the first victim?"

In response, Mueller slapped a thick folder onto the table, its contents slightly spilling out. Morgan reached for it, her fingers brushing against the worn edges of the folder. As she flipped through the pages, Derik leaned in closer, their shoulders touching as they both examined the information.

"Charlesberg," Morgan murmured, her gaze locked on a case from a few years prior. It detailed a disturbingly similar situation – a woman found dead in her new home with no signs of forced entry.

"Charlesberg is a wealthy suburb," Mueller explained, his voice echoing through the room. "It's become quite popular among those looking to escape the chaos of Dallas without straying too far. The real estate market there is booming – always building new homes, attracting big money."

Morgan absently traced the edge of a photograph depicting Charlesberg's picturesque streets, her mind working quickly to piece together any connections between the two cases. She could feel Derik's presence beside her, the warmth radiating from his body as he studied the files alongside her. There was something about this case that had them both on edge, and she couldn't shake the feeling that they were diving headfirst into dangerous territory.

"Are we thinking this is a serial killer?" Derik asked, voicing the question that lingered in the air between them.

"Maybe," Mueller replied, his expression unreadable. "But that's what we need you to find out."

Morgan's eyes flicked to the photograph of Jennifer Stacy, the first victim. The woman's radiant smile seemed out of place in the somber atmosphere of the room. Morgan's fingers traced the outline of the widow's face, noticing the subtle lines of heartbreak etched within her features.

"Jennifer Stacy," she read aloud, her voice heavy with the weight of responsibility. "Divorced a rich man in Dallas, moved to Charlesberg after collecting a hefty sum. Found dead in her new home."

"Her ex-husband had an ironclad alibi," Mueller added, watching Morgan closely. "They couldn't pin anything on him, and no other suspects were found, as you'll see in the file. The case went cold."

"Then Sarah Benson came along, years later," Derik murmured, his gaze lingering on the second victim's picture. She had been young and vibrant, her eyes full of hope.

"Sarah's story is different," Morgan continued, flipping through the file as she absorbed every detail. "Moved to Charlesberg for a new job at a tech company. Social media manager." She paused, allowing the stark contrast between the two women's lives to sink in. "But their deaths... they're almost identical."

"Both struck multiple times in the back of the head with a heavy object," Mueller confirmed, his expression darkening. "No signs of forced entry. It's like the killer just waltzed right into their homes and left without a trace."

"Two different lives, same brutal end," Derik muttered, shaking his head. "What could possibly connect these women?"

Morgan felt a shiver run down her spine as she considered the possibilities. What if there was no connection? What if the killer was indiscriminate, choosing victims based on opportunity rather than any personal vendetta?

"Or maybe," she thought aloud, "the connection isn't obvious. Maybe it's something more subtle, hidden beneath the surface."

Morgan's eyes traced the chaos in the photographs with intensity; the wine glasses scattered around, half-empty, and crumbs of appetizers on plates. She leaned closer to inspect a beer can resting on the coffee table amidst the sea of wine glasses. Her brow furrowed as she considered the implications.

"Derik," she said quietly, her voice edged with frustration, "what if the killer was already inside during the party? Hiding in plain sight?"

Derik glanced over at the photograph, his green eyes narrowing. "It's possible," he admitted reluctantly. "But then how did they escape? All the doors were locked from the inside, and Sarah's house keys were accounted for."

Morgan chewed her lip, racing through scenarios as she shifted her weight from one foot to the other.

"And what about that window?" Derik asked, pointing to another photograph.

Morgan stared at the image, her heart skipping a beat. A small window was left slightly ajar, but it was far too tiny for any adult to squeeze through. She shook her head, feeling a mix of confusion and determination. This murder felt impossible, but she knew there had to be an explanation.

"Dammit," she muttered under her breath, her tattooed fingers gripping the edge of the table as she tried to make sense of it all. "I need to see the crime scene myself."

"Agreed," Derik replied, his expression mirroring her own frustration. "Let's go."

As they stood up to leave, Morgan's thoughts briefly drifted to Skunk, wondering if he was still alive. But she quickly refocused on the task at hand. There would be time to worry about her missing dog later, she told herself.

Right now, she had a murderer to catch.

CHAPTER THREE

Morgan gripped the steering wheel, her knuckles turning white as she navigated the curves of the highway. Derik sat in the passenger seat, his green eyes staring out the window at the blur of passing trees. The silence between them felt heavy but necessary. Morgan's mind raced with thoughts of Skunk and Thomas's betrayal. She focused on the road, determined not to let her personal life interfere with the case at hand.

In the distance, Charlesberg's welcome sign loomed closer. A small, affluent suburb outside of Dallas, its quiet streets would soon be disrupted by their investigation. As they drove past immaculate lawns and large homes, Morgan couldn't help but think about the sinister secret hidden beneath the picturesque façade. Two successful women, Jennifer and Sarah, murdered years apart, and the connection was still unclear.

Derik cleared his throat, breaking the silence. "Morgan, I just wanted to say... I admire your strength. With everything going on, it's a lot for one person to carry."

Morgan's lips tightened into a thin line, acknowledging his words without taking her eyes off the road. She knew Derik was right; with her dog kidnapped by Thomas and the FBI's trustworthiness in question, it was difficult to know who to rely on.

Morgan glanced at Derik briefly before returning her gaze to the road. "I'm just doing what I've always done, Derik - keeping on living. I may be anxious, but I can't let it consume me." Her fingers drummed nervously on the steering wheel as she thought of Skunk, waiting for Thomas to get back to her. "I hope that collar he left at my house was just part of his sick game. If there's one thing I know about Thomas Grady, it's that he likes to rattle me. But I still don't know what his endgame is."

As they drove past the population sign of Carlsberg, the world outside their car window transformed into an idyllic scene of neatly trimmed lawns and beautiful suburban homes. Each house seemed to boast a more impressive garden or grander facade than the last, and

Morgan felt a chill run down her spine. She knew that beneath this picture-perfect exterior, a sinister secret lay hidden.

"Two successful women," she said softly, "Jennifer and now Sarah, murdered years apart. And we still don't know what connects them."

As they continued driving through the picturesque suburb of Charlesberg, Morgan couldn't shake the heavy feeling in her chest. She knew that finding the truth would not only bring justice to the victims but might also untangle the web of deceit that had ensnared her life. With each passing moment, she felt the urgency to solve this case and protect those around her.

Morgan’s car glided to a stop in front of Sarah Benson's newly acquired home. The afternoon sun cast long shadows across the immaculate lawn, highlighting the stark contrast between the vibrant green grass and the pristine white facade. Morgan studied the house, noting the absence of personal touches that would make it feel like a home rather than just a piece of real estate.

"Such a shame," she muttered under her breath, her gaze lingering on the empty flowerbeds waiting for blooms that would never come. "Sarah never got the chance to make this place hers."

Derik nodded silently, his gaze filled with empathy as he took in the scene. Morgan knew all too well the importance of having a sanctuary, a place to call home. And now, Sarah's sanctuary had become her tomb.

Together, they exited the car and approached the cluster of officers already at the scene. A cacophony of police radios and hushed conversations buzzed around them as the investigation began to unfold.

"Agent Morgan Cross, FBI," Morgan introduced herself, flashing her badge confidently. "This is my partner, Agent Derik Greene."

"Thank you for coming," one of the officers said, his face etched with relief at their arrival. "We suspect this case may be connected to the previous one."

"Thank you for calling us," Morgan replied, her voice taking on a steely resolve as she mentally prepared herself to dive into yet another grisly crime scene. She couldn't help but think about Skunk, wondering if Thomas Grady was playing another twisted game with her life. She shook the thought from her mind.

"Let's get to work, Derik," she said quietly, her determination evident in every word. She knew there was no time to waste – not when a killer was still at large, and the sinister threads of her own past were slowly being unraveled with each new discovery.

Morgan stepped over the threshold, her eyes scanning the impeccable interior. The scent of fresh paint still clung to the air, mingling with the subtle aroma of new furniture. She could detect a faint hint of lemon-scented cleaner beneath it all, a reminder that Sarah Benson had barely had time to settle in.

"Agent Cross," a tall officer greeted her, offering a nod and a handshake. "Welcome to the scene."

"Thank you," she replied, taking in the pristine surroundings. Despite the chaos outside, the inside of the house was eerily calm. Officers moved about deliberately, their footsteps muffled by the plush carpet beneath them.

Morgan's gaze drifted through the open archway to the living room, where the heart of this tragedy unfolded. She steeled herself before stepping into the space, her heart rate increasing ever so slightly. It was a sight she'd seen before, but that didn't make it any easier to bear.

Sarah Benson lay sprawled on the floor, her head brutally bashed in, creating a stark contrast against the clean, white carpet. Morgan forced herself to analyze the scene dispassionately. The killer had been fastidious in every other aspect of the crime – no forced entry, no signs of struggle – yet the act itself was anything but.

Why would someone go to such great lengths to enter and exit without leaving a trace, only to commit such a messy murder?

"Whoever did this managed to slip in and out without disturbing anything," Morgan said to Derik. "But the actual murder? It's like they wanted it to be messy."

Derik furrowed his brow, nodding in agreement. "That is strange. It's like they're sending a message."

"Or leaving a signature," Morgan mused, her eyes narrowing as she considered the implications. The killer may have been careful, but they were far from perfect. And it was that imperfection, that trace of humanity, which would ultimately lead to their undoing.

Morgan stepped out of the pristine living room and made her way around the house, examining each door that led to the outside. The side door was smooth and unmarred, its lock untouched, just like the back door and the front door. All were locked from the inside, a puzzle that gnawed at the edges of her mind.

She turned her attention to the windows, finding them all secured except for one small one, left slightly ajar. It was too small for an adult human to fit through—barely large enough for a child or a pet. Morgan's fingers deftly traced the edges of the window, searching for any hidden clues. Her mind raced, considering possibilities: how could someone have bypassed these locks without leaving a visible trace?

"Hey," Derik said softly as he approached her by the side door. He looked pale, visibly disturbed by the crime scene they had just left behind. "What are you thinking?"

Morgan didn't take her eyes off the door. "I want these locks tested for any signs of tampering. I'm convinced the killer left something behind. Not sure what yet, but it's worth looking into."

Derik nodded. "I'll get someone on it right away."

"Thanks," she replied, her gaze still locked on the seemingly undisturbed lock. She felt a shiver run down her spine as she pondered the implications. This killer seemed to be playing a twisted game of cat and mouse, leaving subtle breadcrumbs for them to follow. But why? And where would it lead?

Either way, she would not let this killer slip through her fingers. No matter how many locks they bypassed or how many crime scenes they left spotless, Morgan Cross would be the one to bring them down. And she wouldn't rest until she had unraveled their every secret.

CHAPTER FOUR

Morgan took a breath, standing on the doorstep of Sarah's neighbor's house with Derik at her side. In order to understand who'd killed Sarah—and why—they had to gather as much information as they could. Morgan's heart clenched as she thought about the gruesome scene they had just left behind, hidden amongst the picturesque suburban facade.

"Ready?" Derik asked, his hand poised to knock on the door. Morgan nodded, and he rapped sharply on the wooden surface.

The door swung open to reveal a young couple, the woman cradling a small child in her arms. Morgan's breath caught at the sight of the innocent toddler, no older than two, so close to a murder scene. The child stared at them with wide, curious eyes, blissfully unaware of the horrors that had occurred nearby.

"Hello," Morgan began, forcing a smile. "I'm Special Agent Morgan Cross, and this is my partner, Special Agent Derik Greene. We're with the FBI."

"Hi," the man said, taking a step forward to shake their hands. "I'm Eric Wilson, and this is my wife, Amy, and our son, Jake."

"Nice to meet you," Morgan replied, fighting the urge to glance back at Sarah's house. "I'm sure you heard what happened next door."

"Of course," Amy said, her voice shaking slightly. "We didn't know her very well, but it's terrible what happened. We'd just made a pie for her as a welcome gift, but now..." She trailed off, tears filling her eyes. "If there's anything we can do to help, please let us know."

"Thank you for offering your help," Derik said, his voice gentle. "Did you notice anything unusual last night during the party at Sarah's house? Any unfamiliar faces or suspicious activity?"

"Sarah had mentioned inviting friends and family from Dallas," Eric explained. "We didn't know any of them, so it's hard to say who was unfamiliar or suspicious."

"Everyone seemed friendly enough," Amy added, her gaze fixed on the child in her arms. "I can't believe someone would do something like that to her. She was so excited to start a new life here."

Morgan sighed inwardly, knowing their task wouldn't be easy. The killer had left almost no trace behind, and now they were faced with a sea of seemingly innocent faces. But she would not give up. She refused to let this monster continue to prey on unsuspecting victims.

Morgan's dark eyes swept the immaculate lawn and manicured hedges of Charlesberg as she considered their next move. "Did you see anyone unfamiliar lurking around yesterday?" She asked, her voice low and focused. "Or any strange activity?"

Eric scratched his chin thoughtfully, a furrow creasing his brow. "We only met Sarah ourselves one time, and that was yesterday when she told us about the party. She mentioned inviting friends and family from Dallas."

Morgan mentally filed away this information, remembering the police had already interviewed and cleared those guests. She needed something more to go on, something that could lead her closer to the murderer.

"Because we didn't know any of them," Amy cut in, nervously adjusting her grip on the child, "it's hard to say who could have been suspicious. But there was this one guy we saw on the street earlier in the day before the party even started. We'd never seen him around here before."

"Can you describe him?" Derik asked, his green eyes narrowing.

Amy hesitated, glancing at her husband for support. "He didn't look like he was from around here. I mean, he was dressed sort of... homely."

Morgan weighed the couple's words carefully. Could this be their first real lead? Her pulse quickened at the possibility. Every small detail mattered, and the stranger's presence in an affluent neighborhood like Charlesberg seemed out of place.

"Is there anything else you can tell us about this man?" Morgan asked, hoping to glean more information from Amy and Eric.

"Sorry, that's all we know," Amy said with a sigh. "He could be no one, just someone who wandered into the neighborhood."

"Or he could be someone," Derik added quietly.

"Right," Morgan agreed. She made a mental note of the stranger as a potential lead. "Thank you for your help."

"Of course, Agent Cross," Eric replied, his voice filled with concern. "If we think of anything else, we'll make sure to contact you."

"Please do," Morgan said, offering them a reassuring smile before she and Derik turned to leave.

As they walked back to Sarah Benson's house, Morgan's nerves rose. The investigation was moving forward, but time was of the essence. Every moment that passed meant another opportunity for the killer to slip through their fingers.

"Those interviews with the friends and family from Dallas should be done by now," Derik mentioned as they approached the crime scene.

"Let's find out," Morgan said, her eyes scanning the officers still present. She spotted a familiar face and called out to him. "Officer Davis, have those interviews been completed?"

"Yes, Agent Cross," Officer Davis replied, holding a clipboard in his hand. "We've looked into the whereabouts of every person confirmed at the parties, and found they all returned to Dallas as they'd said."

"Good work," Morgan nodded, her brow furrowing as she considered the implications of this information. If everyone at the party had been accounted for, then the stranger Amy and Eric had seen earlier in the day took on even greater significance.

"Thanks, Officer Davis," Derik said, his expression matching Morgan's seriousness. "Keep us updated if you learn anything new."

"Will do, Agent Greene," Davis responded before walking away to continue his duties.

Morgan's mind buzzed with thoughts as she processed the information they had gathered so far. Every detail mattered. The stranger in the neighborhood, Sarah's friends and family from Dallas, and the locked doors with no signs of tampering - all pieces of a puzzle she was determined to solve.

"Come on," she said to Derik, her voice resolute. "There's more work to be done."

Morgan's eyes scanned the room, taking in every detail of the crime scene before her. The crimson splatters on the pristine white walls seemed to mock the idea of safety within one's home. Amidst the chaos of the bloody aftermath, a lone beer can glinted in the dim light, perched on the coffee table like a trophy.

"Officer," Morgan called out, her voice steady despite the gruesome sight before her. "This was a wine party, wasn't it? So, who brought in the beer?"

The officer glanced at the can and shook his head. "I don't know, Agent Cross. We haven't questioned the partygoers about that."

"Then get statements from all of them. I want to know who brought it," Morgan insisted, her gut telling her there was more to this seemingly innocuous item than met the eye.

"Are you sure?" the officer asked, skepticism clear in his tone. "Seems pretty straightforward - someone at the party didn't like wine, so they brought their own drink."

"Look," Morgan said, her voice firm as she locked eyes with the officer. "Earlier today, our neighbors saw a strange man skulking around the area. I want every small detail accounted for. It may be nothing, but we need to leave no stone unturned."

The officer nodded and left Morgan and Derik standing alone in the hushed crime scene. As the silence settled around them, Morgan's gaze traveled over the untampered locks, the mysterious beer can, and the lingering memory of the strange man that haunted her thoughts. These three clues were the key to finding Sarah's killer, and Morgan knew she needed to focus on deciphering their hidden messages before it was too late.

"Derik, let's regroup at the precinct and dive into the old files," she said, her voice resolute as she met his eyes. "We need to find a pattern, something that connects these cases."

***

Morgan found herself alone in the briefing room at the local police precinct. The dim lighting cast eerie shadows on the walls as she spread out the cold case files from Jennifer's murder years earlier. Her fingers traced the worn edges of the documents, the somber weight of history pressing down upon her like a heavy cloak.

As she compared the details of Jennifer's case with those of Sarah's, Morgan became acutely aware of the similarities that seemed to tie the two crimes together. It was unnerving, unsettling - but also undeniable. She needed to find the connection, the thread that would unravel this twisted tapestry and reveal the face of the monster who had taken two innocent lives.

"Focus, Morgan," she whispered to herself, feeling the exhaustion creeping up on her as the hours ticked by. But she couldn't afford to rest, not while Sarah's killer still lurked in the shadows.

Her concentration was interrupted as Derik entered the room, carrying two cups of steaming coffee. Setting one down in front of

Morgan, he pulled up a chair beside her and began flipping through the files as well.

"Any breakthroughs?" he asked, his voice tinged with hope.

"Nothing concrete yet," Morgan admitted, her frustration apparent. "But there has to be something here, Derik. Some detail we're overlooking."

"Let's keep digging," he encouraged, taking a sip of his coffee as they dove back into the cold files together, determined to unearth the truth that lay buried beneath layers of darkness and deceit.

Morgan's eyes strained from pouring over the documents and photographs that cluttered the table before her. She tried to discern a pattern in the killer's methods. It was almost as if he were a ghost, slipping into these women's homes undetected, committing his heinous acts, and then vanishing without a trace, leaving the doors locked from the inside out.

"Come on," she muttered, frustration gnawing at her resolve. "There has to be something."

As she flipped through the crime scene photographs of Jennifer's case, a glint caught her eye. In one image, taken from a distance, she saw it: a beer can that looked strikingly similar to the one found at Sarah's crime scene. Her pulse quickened as she shuffled through the photos, finally finding the close-up shot of the can.

"Derik," she called, her voice urgent, "come take a look at this."

Derik walked over, his brow furrowing as he studied the photograph. "It's just a beer can, Morgan. What's so special about it?"

"Look at it, Derik," she insisted, tapping her finger against the image. "It's practically identical to the one we found at Sarah's. And none of her guests claimed ownership of it."

"Okay," Derik conceded, "but it could still be a coincidence, right? People drink beer all the time."

"Sure, people drink beer," Morgan replied, "but how many of them bring their own can to a wine party, then leave it behind at a murder scene?"

"Alright, let's say you're onto something," Derik said, leaning in closer and scrutinizing the photo. "What does it tell us about the killer?"

Morgan drummed her fingers on the table, her gaze never leaving the photograph. "I'm not sure yet," she admitted. "But if this is more than a coincidence, it could be the break we need to catch this bastard."

"Let's keep digging," Derik urged, his voice filled with determination. "If there's a connection here, we'll find it."

As they returned their focus to the files before them, Morgan couldn't shake the feeling that they were on the verge of something monumental. It was a hunch, but a strong one – and Morgan's instincts rarely led her astray.

Morgan narrowed her eyes at the two images of beer cans, their colorful labels shimmering under the harsh fluorescent lights. Both tall cans, craft beer from different breweries, yet eerily similar in the context of two murder scenes. She clenched her jaw, her gut churning with the sense that there was something more to this. Rising abruptly from her chair, she strode out into the bustling police precinct.

"Officer," she called out, her voice cutting through the din of ringing phones and muffled conversations. A young officer glanced up from his desk, acknowledging her with a nod. "Has everyone from the party been contacted regarding the beer can?"

The officer sighed, rubbing his tired eyes. "Yes, ma'am. Just finished calling them all again. Took a while, what with so many people there, and some are still pretty shaken up."

"Did anyone claim responsibility for bringing in the beer?" Morgan asked.

"Strange thing is," he replied, his brow furrowed, "not a single person admitted to it."

Morgan's pulse quickened, her mind racing. Could this be the clue they needed? That one loose thread to unravel the killer's identity? She thanked the officer and made her way back to the briefing room, her dark hair swaying with purpose.

"Derik," she said as she entered the room, slamming the photos onto the table. "No one from the party claimed to have brought in the beer."

"Really?" Derik raised an eyebrow, his interest piqued. "So what now?"

"We need to find out if there's any connection between these cans." Morgan tapped her fingers on the table, her thoughts swirling like storm clouds. "Because if there is, we might just be able to catch this bastard."

"Alright," Derik agreed, determination etched in the lines of his face. "Let's get to work."

As they delved back into the case files, Morgan could feel it deep in her bones: that intuitive certainty that had guided her through countless investigations. This beer can was more than just a random piece of evidence – it was the key to unlocking the truth behind these chilling murders.

CHAPTER FIVE

When Morgan returned to the briefing room, she found Derik entering from the opposite side, arms laden with takeout containers.

"Thought you could use some sustenance," he said, kicking the door shut behind him.

"Thanks." Morgan glanced at the food but shook her head. "But there's more work to do. None of Sarah's guests claimed ownership over that beer can."

"Got it." Derik set the containers on the table and began unpacking them. He pulled out a burger and took a bite, looking thoughtful. "So what? It's just beer."

"Look." Morgan flipped open one of the case files to reveal a photo from Jennifer's crime scene, revealing an eerily similar beer can in the background.

Derik frowned, clearly disturbed. "Are you suggesting this could be the killer's calling card?"

"Maybe." Morgan stared at the images, her eyes flicking between the two cans. "I'm not sure yet, but my gut is telling me there's something here."

"Your gut has a good track record." Derik paused, eyeing her with concern. "But you need to eat, too. Can't solve crimes on an empty stomach."

"Alright, alright." Morgan reluctantly grabbed a container of fries, still focused on the photographs. As she chewed mechanically, her thoughts churned, weaving together strands of possibility.

"Let's run with your theory for now," Derik suggested, his voice cautious but supportive. "What's our next step?"

"First," Morgan replied, determination hardening her resolve, "we find out if there's any connection between these cans – anything that could lead us to the killer."

"Agreed." Derik's green eyes flashed with renewed purpose. "Let's get to work."

Sighing, Morgan slid into the chair across from Derik, her fingers brushing against the slightly greasy wrapper of a burger. The aroma of cooked beef and melted cheese wafted through the air as she hesitated, torn between satisfying her hunger and delving deeper into the case. Just then, her phone buzzed on the table, abruptly pulling her attention away from the meal.

"Agent Cross," she answered, her voice steady despite the anticipation that tightened in her chest. "What do you have for me, Dr. Smith?"

"Ah, Agent Cross." The coroner's tone was grave, his words measured. "The toxicology report for Sarah Benson came back, and I thought it best to discuss it with you directly."

"Go on," Morgan urged, her eyes flicking to Derik who had paused mid-bite, his own curiosity piqued.

"An unknown substance was found in Ms. Benson's bloodstream," Dr. Smith revealed, his voice tinged with confusion. "It appears to be some sort of drug, but we can't identify it just yet."

Morgan's mind raced, sifting through potential implications and connections. Was this somehow linked to the mysterious beer cans? She clenched her free hand into a fist, frustrated by the lingering questions.

"Thank you, Dr. Smith," she said, her voice betraying a hint of her urgency. "Please call me as soon as you know more about this substance."

"Of course, Agent Cross. I'll keep you informed."

As Morgan hung up, the weight of the new information pressed heavily upon her. She looked at Derik, his furrowed brow mirroring her own concerns.

"Sarah Benson had an unknown drug in her system," she shared, her mind already churning with theories and possible connections.

"Could it be related to the beer cans?" Derik mused aloud, his appetite momentarily forgotten.

"Maybe," Morgan replied, her gaze drifting to the photos strewn across the table. "But first, we need to find out more about this substance and what it could mean for our investigation."

"Right," Derik agreed, his eyes locked onto hers with unwavering support. "We'll get to the bottom of this, Morgan. Together."

Morgan's grip on her phone tightened as she ended the call, her pulse quickening. The dimly lit room seemed to close in around her, the cold files scattered across the table like ghosts of the past. Derik watched her with concern etched into his handsome features, the remains of their meal momentarily forgotten. She locked eyes with him, her resolve steeling in the face of this new challenge.

"Derik, we need to get the lab to run tests on that beer can left behind," she said, her voice unwavering despite the whirlwind of thoughts swirling within her. "We can't afford to waste any more time."

"Agreed," Derik replied, pushing aside the remnants of their dinner and rising from his chair. "Let's go."

As they strode through the bustling precinct, Morgan felt a renewed sense of purpose. Every step brought her closer to unraveling the twisted web of deceit and violence that had ensnared both Jennifer and Sarah – and perhaps countless others. Her fingers itched for answers, for something tangible to grasp onto amidst the chaos.

"Hey, Morgan," Derik said, breaking through her reverie as they approached the door to the forensic lab. "We've got this. We'll find the truth – for them, and for ourselves."

His words washed over her like a balm, soothing the raw edges of her anxiety. For a moment, she allowed herself to lean into the support he offered, the knowledge that, despite everything, they were in this together.

"Thank you, Derik," she murmured, opening the door and stepping into the sterile, white-walled lab. A technician looked up from their work, curiosity piqued by their sudden arrival.

"Agent Cross," they greeted, adjusting their glasses. "What can I do for you?"

"We need you to run tests on this beer can found at Sarah Benson's crime scene," Morgan explained, her voice brimming with authority. "We believe it may be connected to both her murder and that of Jennifer Mitchell."

"Of course," the technician replied, nodding solemnly. "I'll do everything I can to help."

"Thank you," Morgan said, exchanging a glance with Derik as they left the lab. The weight of their mission settled heavily on her shoulders, but she knew that, together, they would face whatever darkness lay ahead.

For now, all they could do was wait, trust in their instincts, and hope that the answers they sought would finally come to light.

***

Morgan stood beside Derik, her gaze fixed on the scientists in their white lab coats, hunched over microscopes and test tubes. The sterile smell of the local lab hung in the air, mingling with her growing impatience. Her dark hair was pulled back into a tight ponytail, revealing tattoos snaking up her neck and down her arms – a reminder of the years she spent behind bars for a crime she didn't commit.

"Any luck with the forensic DNA?" Morgan asked, trying to keep the edge out of her voice. "Anything that indicates drugs or chemicals at the scene?"

A lab tech shook his head, not bothering to look up from his work. "Nothing so far, Agent Cross. We're still running tests."

"Keep me updated," Morgan said, clenching her jaw as she turned her attention to another technician. "What about the beer can found near the body? Any DNA evidence?"

The technician frowned, scrolling through data on a tablet. "Actually, we didn't find any traces of saliva on the can. It's like no one even drank from it."

"Damn it." Morgan rubbed the bridge of her nose, her frustration mounting. Beside her, Derik shifted uneasily, his green eyes betraying a shared sense of helplessness.

"Could it be just a coincidence?" Derik suggested, his voice tinged with exhaustion. "Maybe it's unrelated to the murder?"

"Maybe," Morgan replied, unconvinced. She glanced around the lab, watching the flurry of activity. "But nothing is ever simple in cases like this."

"True." Derik sighed, running a hand through his slick black hair. He looked tired, the weight of their investigation pressing down on him. His battle with alcoholism and the strain of his divorce had left him worn thin, but he remained determined to find the truth. "We'll figure it out, Morgan."

"Damn right, we will," she muttered, more to herself than to Derik. They had been through so much together, and despite his past betrayal, she was starting to trust him again. But trust didn't make this case any easier.

As they continued to watch the technicians work, Morgan couldn't help but feel a gnawing sense of dread. This case was proving to be more complex than she'd anticipated, and with each passing moment, the stakes felt higher. She needed answers, and she needed them soon – before the killer struck again.

The weight of frustration threatened to crush Morgan as she stepped out into the cool night air. The darkness outside only seemed to echo the darkness within her thoughts, and she inhaled deeply, trying to clear her mind. She glanced down at her phone, the screen casting a pale glow on her tattooed hands. Still no word from Thomas, the man she once considered a friend, now a tormentor holding her beloved dog, Skunk, hostage.

"Hey," Derik's voice sounded behind her, his footsteps crunching on the gravel as he approached. "You okay?"

Morgan looked up at him, her dark eyes reflecting the strain of their fruitless day. "No, I'm not okay. We've been here all day, and we still don't have a solid suspect." She clenched her fists tightly, feeling the anger bubbling just beneath the surface. "And Thomas... that bastard is still playing games with me."

Derik placed a comforting hand on her shoulder, his green eyes filled with empathy. "I know it's hard, but remember, the team is working overtime on the samples. Everyone is doing their best."

Morgan sighed, realizing he was right. They were all tired, and pushing themselves wouldn't necessarily yield results any faster. "Yeah, you're right. Maybe we should find a spot to crash for the night."

"Good idea," Derik agreed, offering her a weary smile. "We could both use some rest. Let's find a hotel and get some sleep. Tomorrow's a new day."

As they walked back toward the lab to gather their things, Morgan found herself clinging to the hope that tomorrow would bring the answers they so desperately needed. But in the shadows of her mind, doubt and fear continued to haunt her, whispering that time was running out.

CHAPTER SIX

Morgan's gut churned as she stepped into the dimly lit hotel lobby, Derik beside her. The faint scent of lemon-scented cleaner mixed with musty air hung around them as they approached the reception desk. A middle-aged woman with a worn smile greeted them, her fingers tapping at the computer keyboard.

"Good evening," she said, her eyes flicking up to meet theirs. "How can I help you?"

"Two rooms, please," Morgan requested, her voice strained from exhaustion. She hoped that by distancing herself from Derik for the night, she could find some semblance of peace to face the next day's challenges.

"I'm sorry, but we're all booked up," the receptionist replied apologetically. "There's not much tourism in Charlesberg, so we only have a few rooms. We do have one room available with a bed, though."

Morgan clenched her jaw, cursing her luck. The thought of sharing a room with Derik made her stomach twist, but it was late, and they needed rest. Swallowing her pride, she nodded. "We'll take it."

"Here's your key," the receptionist handed over a small plastic card. "The room is on the second floor, number 203. Enjoy your stay."

"Thanks," Morgan muttered, turning to leave the lobby with Derik following silently behind. As they climbed the carpeted stairs, memories of their previous partnership before the betrayal surfaced, further stirring her unease.

Reaching the door to room 203, she hesitated for a moment before swiping the keycard and pushing it open. A soft click echoed through the narrow hallway as the lock disengaged. The room was modestly furnished, the muted colors of the bedspread and curtains providing little comfort to the tense atmosphere.

Morgan sighed quietly, her thoughts racing. Sharing a room with Derik brought back memories of when they were closer, but now their relationship was fractured, and it made her uneasy. As she set her bag down on the bed, she reminded herself that this was just one night, and then they'd be back to work.

The door clicked shut behind them, sealing the pair into the confines of room 203.

"Look, I'll just sleep on the couch," Derik said, dropping his bag beside it with a soft thud. His green eyes flicked over to Morgan briefly, gauging her reaction.

"Fine." She didn't argue, her mind too preoccupied with the case. She knew that Derik was trying to make things easier between them — an unspoken apology lingering in the air — but she couldn't push down the unease completely. Being so close to him after everything wasn't going to be easy.

Morgan pulled out her phone once more, hoping for some news from Thomas. But as before, there was nothing. Her fingers drummed against the screen, frustration mounting. How could he have just vanished? And what if he had hurt Skunk?

"Are you sure you don't want to get the FBI involved now?" Derik asked, cautious concern lacing his voice. "I know you can't trust them, but—"

"Exactly," Morgan snapped, cutting him off. "I can't trust them."

"But not everyone in the FBI wanted you framed for murder," Derik insisted, his tone gentle yet persistent. "There are people who can help. What if Thomas has already hurt your dog?"

His words struck a chord within her, and she bit her lip, torn between her instincts and her fears. Her resolve wavered, and for a moment, she considered his suggestion. But ultimately, she shook her head.

Morgan's frustration boiled over. "Involving others is risky, Derik," she grunted, pacing the limited floor space of their cramped hotel room. "You know why Thomas went off the grid? Because he saw you coming to my house."

Derik ran a hand through his slick black hair, his eyes clouded with concern. "I know," he replied quietly, rubbing the back of his neck wearily. "But what other options do we have?"

"Let me think," Morgan snapped, halting her pacing and glaring at him.

"Fine," Derik sighed, holding up his hands in surrender. "Take your time."

"Right now, I need a shower," she muttered, stalking toward the bathroom. "And some space to think."

"Sure thing," Derik said, stepping aside to let her pass.

The door clicked shut behind her, and Morgan wasted no time in dialing Thomas's number. The phone rang, then went straight to voicemail. He was ignoring her... damn. As the water heated up, Morgan leaned against the cool tiles, feeling the weight of her decisions bearing down on her shoulders. What if Derik was right? Maybe this was much bigger than her, and if she wanted to save Skunk's life, maybe she had no choice but to involve the FBI.

As the steam began to fill the bathroom, Morgan stared at her reflection in the foggy mirror, her dark hair damp with sweat from the day's events. Her tattoos seemed to blur together, a tapestry of ink that told a story of pain, betrayal, and resilience.

She couldn't risk losing everything again, but the thought of Skunk suffering at Thomas's hands twisted her insides into knots.

The shower hissed as Morgan pushed the thought of involving the FBI aside and stepped under the steaming water. It washed over her, a torrential downpour that seemed to carry away the stress that had burrowed into her bones. She closed her eyes, allowing herself this brief reprieve from reality.

"Damn it, Thomas," she whispered, her voice barely audible above the roar of the water.

As her thoughts drifted to the case, the gruesome images of Sarah Benson's body resurfaced in her mind, sending a shudder through her that had nothing to do with the temperature. The sight of Sarah's mutilated corpse haunted her, leaving a heavy feeling in the pit of her stomach that coiled into dread.

"Is it really him?" she muttered to herself, raking her fingers through her wet hair. "The same killer from years ago?" If so, then his timeline was stretched out, making it impossible to predict when — or if — he would strike again. The thought of another person dying in such a horrible way made her stomach churn.

As the water flowed over her, she tried to hold onto that hope. But with no forensic data, pinpointing a suspect seemed nearly impossible. The feeling of helplessness gnawed at her, threatening to consume her.

Damn it all, she thought, thumping her fist against the cold tiles. *We can't let another life be taken by this monster.*

Turning off the shower, she stepped out of the stall, her body slick and dripping. She wrapped herself in a towel and stared at her reflection in the mirror. Her dark eyes were haunted, betraying the fear and determination that roiled within her. Morgan knew she couldn't hesitate any longer.

Tomorrow, we'll find something, she vowed to herself, her voice firm and resolute. "And if it's the last thing I do, I'll make sure this killer is stopped."

For now, though, all she could do was hope that a good night's sleep would bring clarity and renewed energy.

Morgan stepped out of the steaming shower, water dripping from her body. She dried off and threw on some nightwear, then reached for her phone. The screen lit up, revealing an unread text message from an unknown number. She frowned, a sense of unease creeping up her spine as she read the words.

So *far, you've passed this test. Not involving the FBI has been smart. Your dog is still alive... for now. I'll see you soon, Morgan.*

Her blood ran cold, and she gritted her teeth in anger. There was no doubt that the message was from Thomas, taunting her with Skunk's life hanging in the balance. Rage simmered beneath her skin as she hastily pulled on her clothes, fingers fumbling with the buttons of her shirt.

"Derik!" she called out, storming into the main room where he lounged on the couch, clad in his nightwear. His eyes widened in surprise at her sudden appearance. "Look at this."

She thrust the phone toward him, and as he read the text, his expression shifted from confusion to fury. "That sadistic bastard," he muttered through clenched teeth.

"I know," Morgan agreed, the fire within her stoked by his shared anger. "But we have to play his game for now. If we don't, Skunk's as good as dead."

Derik nodded, understanding the gravity of their situation. "Alright, but we'll find a way to turn the tables on him. We won't let him keep holding all the cards."

In that moment, Morgan felt grateful for Derik's support. Despite the cracks in their relationship, they were united in their determination to rescue Skunk and bring Thomas to justice. But first, they had to endure his twisted games and hope for an opportunity to strike back.

"Let's get some rest," Morgan suggested, trying to steady her frayed nerves. "We'll need all our strength for whatever he throws at us next, and for the case."

"Agreed," Derik said, settling back onto the couch. He turned off the lamp, plunging the room into darkness.

As Morgan lay on the bed, thoughts of Skunk and Thomas plagued her, making sleep elusive. She had no choice but to play this dangerous game, but she vowed to herself that she would win – no matter the cost.

***

The first rays of sunlight pierced through a gap in the curtains, casting a warm glow on the hotel room's walls. Morgan stirred, her eyelids fluttering open as she was pulled from the depths of a rare, blissful dream. In that fleeting world, Skunk had been with her again, Thomas had vanished, and life was good.

As wakefulness took hold, the pain of reality set in – the dream was just a cruel illusion. A heavy sigh escaped her lips as she rose from the bed, the lingering warmth of her dream fading away. She felt a pang of envy for those who slept peacefully, unburdened by nightmares or tormenting dreams.

"Derik?" she called out, realizing he wasn't in the room. Her voice sounded small, swallowed up by the silence around her. He must have gone out for coffee, she mused, grateful for a moment of privacy to collect herself.

Morgan began to change into her professional attire, pulling on tailored black slacks and reaching for a white blouse. The soft rustle of the door opening caught her attention, and she turned to see Derik entering the room, holding two steaming cups of coffee.

"Sorry!" he exclaimed, averting his eyes as he realized he'd almost caught her mid-change. His cheeks flushed a deep shade of red, a stark contrast to his usual cool composure.

"It's okay," she said, feeling her own face grow warm as she hurriedly finished buttoning up her blouse. "I'm decent now."

"Here," Derik said, offering her a cup of coffee as he approached. "Thought you might need this."

"Thanks," she replied, accepting the cup gratefully and taking a cautious sip. The hot liquid seared her tongue, but the bitterness helped ground her back in reality.

"Anytime," Derik answered, his eyes meeting hers for a brief moment before he turned away, busying himself with his own coffee. "Got us some breakfast, too," Derik announced, setting down a paper bag on the small table in their hotel room. The aroma of freshly brewed coffee mingled with the scent of toasted bagels, momentarily distracting Morgan from the gravity of their situation.

"Thanks," she murmured, taking her seat across from him. The wooden chair creaked beneath her weight as she leaned forward, resting her elbows on the table. "We should go over the files from both cases again, see if we missed any connections."

"Agreed," Derik replied, pulling out his laptop and opening the digital case files. As he scrolled through the evidence, Morgan couldn't help but notice the dark circles under his eyes – a testament to his own struggles, perhaps, or simply a reflection of the long hours they'd been working.

"Did you find anything?" she asked after a few minutes of silent perusal.

"Nothing yet," he admitted, rubbing his temples with the tips of his fingers. "I've been comparing timelines, locations… even the victims' backgrounds. So far, no obvious links."

Morgan sighed, her frustration mounting as she picked up her own coffee cup and took a sip. The bitterness jolted her senses, giving her a much-needed boost of energy. She narrowed her eyes at the screen, determined not to let Thomas's twisted game defeat her.

"Let's keep looking," she said, her voice resolute. "There has to be something we're missing."

"Right," Derik nodded, returning his focus to the task at hand. They worked in tandem, poring over crime scene photos, witness statements, and autopsy reports, searching for the elusive thread that would tie everything together.

As the minutes ticked by, Morgan's stomach churned with a mixture of hunger and anxiety. She tore off a piece of her bagel and forced herself to eat, the dry taste of the bread doing little to alleviate her growing unease.

Morgan's fingers hovered above the keyboard as she skimmed Jennifer's case file once more. A detail caught her eye, one she hadn't noticed before – Jennifer had moved into a new home just prior to her death and had commissioned a local locksmith named Michael Rivers to change the locks. Her heart quickened with renewed purpose.

"Derik," Morgan said, her voice low and urgent. "I think I found something."

His eyes snapped to hers, dark circles beneath them from their relentless investigation. "What is it?"

"Jennifer had her locks changed by a man named Michael Rivers right before she died. If we can find a connection between him and Sarah, we might be onto something."

"Good catch," Derik praised, his tired features lifting in encouragement. "Let's look him up."

Morgan delved into the FBI database on her laptop, pulling up Sarah's phone records from their ongoing investigation. There, buried among countless numbers, was the contact for Michael's shop. Her pulse spiked at the discovery.

"Derik, I found it," she said, her voice trembling with excitement. "Sarah also contacted Michael Rivers about a lock. This could be our missing link."

"Damn. This guy is worth looking into."

"Agreed," she replied. "We need to find him and figure out what he knows."

"Let's hit the road then," Derik said, determination etched in every line of his face. "Michael Rivers won't know what hit him."

As they prepared to leave, Morgan couldn't help but feel a shiver of trepidation snake down her spine. Was Michael Rivers the key to unlocking Thomas's twisted game, or were they simply walking into another trap? She banished the thought, focusing instead on the task at hand – finding Michael Rivers and, with any luck, bringing Skunk home safely.

***

The sun peeked above the horizon, casting a gloomy pall over the streets of Charlesberg as Morgan and Derik approached Michael's locksmith shop. Its grime-covered windows and peeling paint seemed to mirror their growing unease. Morgan's heart pounded in her chest, her dark eyes scanning the area for any signs of danger. Derik, ever the professional, remained stoic but alert, his green eyes narrowing as he surveyed the shop's exterior.

They pushed through the door, a rusty bell heralding their entrance. The dimly lit interior offered little comfort. Rows of keys hung from the walls, glinting like ominous trophies in the weak light. The air was close and musty, tainted with the scent of old metal and dust. Morgan's stomach churned as they descended deeper into the shop.

"Looks like we're alone," Derik whispered, his gaze sweeping over the empty aisles. "Think he's here?"

Morgan shrugged, her thoughts clouded by the weight of the case and her concern for Skunk. "He better be. We need answers."

As they moved deeper into the shop, Morgan couldn't help but notice the eerie stillness that seemed to pervade the space, as if the very walls were holding their breath. Her fingers twitched at her side, itching for her gun, though she knew it would do no good against Thomas or whatever trap he might have set for them.

"Hey," Derik said suddenly, breaking the silence. "Look at this."

He pointed to a display of ornate locks, their intricate mechanisms showcased beneath glass. Morgan frowned at the sight, wondering what kind of person took such pride in their work. She couldn't shake the feeling that there was more to Michael Rivers than met the eye.

"Seems like he's proud of his craftsmanship," she mused, her voice barely a whisper. "But is it enough to connect him to two murders?"

Derik shook his head, his slick black hair falling over his forehead. "Only one way to find out."

With that, they continued their search, the oppressive atmosphere of the shop bearing down on them as they took in every detail, hoping to find some clue to unlock the truth about Michael Rivers and his possible connection to the victims.

As they rounded a corner, the sudden sound of an eerie voice sent a shiver down Morgan's spine. Michael Rivers, a thin, wiry man with a hunched posture, emerged from the shadows, wearing overalls that seemed to blend into the dark recesses of his shop. His eyes darted back and forth between them, as if he could sense their intentions.

"Can I help you folks?" he asked, his voice cracking slightly.

Without missing a beat, Morgan and Derik both held up their badges. "Morgan Cross, FBI," she said, her voice steady despite the unease she felt. "This is my partner, Derik Greene."

Michael's eyes widened as he took in their credentials, his hands starting to tremble ever so slightly. He swallowed hard, clearly nervous about their presence.

"Did you recently change a lock for a woman named Sarah Benson?" Morgan asked, her gaze unyielding as she studied the locksmith.

"Y-yes," Michael stammered, hesitating just long enough for Morgan to notice. "I remember her well. Changed her lock just the other day."

As she listened to his response, Morgan couldn't help but analyze each word, searching for any hint of deception or guilt. She noticed how his fingers fidgeted with the hem of his overalls, betraying his anxiety. Is this the man who killed Sarah? Why would he do it?

"Did she mention anything unusual during your visit?" Derik chimed in. "Anything at all that might give us a clue as to why someone would want her dead?"

Michael shook his head, his hunched posture making him appear smaller than he already was. "No, nothing like that. She just wanted a new lock, said she always did that when she moved into a new place. Seemed pretty normal to me."

Morgan bit the inside of her cheek, frustration boiling beneath the surface. If only she could find a solid lead, something to point them in the right direction. She needed to press him further but had to be careful not to push too hard and scare him off.

"Did you know Sarah personally?" Morgan asked, keeping her voice as neutral as possible. "Any connection between the two of you outside of your professional relationship?"

"Uh, no," Michael replied, his eyes flicking to the side for a moment before meeting Morgan's again. "I just met her when I changed her lock."

Morgan could sense Derik's growing impatience beside her, but she knew they couldn't afford to alienate Michael just yet. They needed more information, and he might be their only link to what happened to Sarah Benson.

Morgan glanced at Derik, who gave her a subtle nod. It was time to push deeper, even if it meant making Michael more uncomfortable. She leaned in slightly, her dark eyes never leaving his face. "Michael, I need you to think back for me. About eight years ago, did you do any work for a woman named Jennifer? Same kind of job – changing locks."

Michael's eyes widened, and he shifted his weight from one foot to the other. He opened his mouth, then closed it again, as if unsure what to say. Morgan could see the gears turning in his head, his pulse quickening beneath the thin skin of his neck. She kept her expression neutral, giving him space to think and respond.

"Jennifer?" he finally said, his voice cracking ever so slightly. "I... I've worked with a lot of people over the years. I can't say for certain."

Morgan steeled herself as she continued, careful not to let her frustration show. "Jennifer's last name was Stacy," she added pointedly. "She was murdered, much like Sarah Benson. We're trying to find any connection between the two victims, and you are the only link we've found so far. Please, try to remember."

Michael's hands began to tremble, and beads of sweat formed on his forehead. He swallowed hard and looked down, avoiding Morgan's gaze. "I... I might have done some work for her. I can't remember all my clients, but... yeah, maybe."

"Did you notice anything unusual about her or her home? Anything that might connect her to Sarah Benson?" Morgan pressed, her voice taking on an edge as she sensed Michael's growing unease.

His breath hitched, and he shook his head adamantly. "No, no. Nothing like that. Just another job. Changed the lock, got paid, and left. That's it."

Morgan could feel the tension in the room crackling like electricity, as if one wrong move would send everything spiraling out of control. She had to find a way to break through Michael's defenses, to dig into his memories and unearth the truth.

Morgan's eyes narrowed as she studied Michael's body language, noting the way he fidgeted with his hands and avoided eye contact. She sensed an underlying fear in him that was growing more pronounced with every question. Her instincts screamed at her to press on, to uncover whatever Michael was hiding.

"Michael," Morgan said softly, trying to keep her voice steady and non-threatening. "I need you to think back. Did anything unusual happen when you changed Jennifer's locks? Did she say or do anything out of the ordinary?"

"Nothing!" Michael snapped, suddenly defensive. "Just a job, like I said. Can't remember much else."

"Come on, there has to be something," Derik chimed in, his eyes boring into Michael.

Feeling cornered, Michael's eyes darted frantically around the room as if searching for an escape route. His entire body tensed up, like a spring wound too tight. Without warning, he lunged toward the counter, grabbing a nearby wrench and brandishing it like a weapon.

"Back off! I don't know anything!" he snarled, panic and desperation evident in his voice.

"Michael, put the wrench down," Morgan ordered, her tone calm yet firm. "You're not helping your case here."

Instead, Michael bolted, knocking over a nearby display of keys and plunging the shop into a cacophony of jangling metal. Morgan and Derik sprang into action, following him as he weaved through the narrow aisles lined with tools and lock components.

Derik lunged forward, attempting to grab Michael's arm, but the wiry man sidestepped him, using his knowledge of the cluttered space to his advantage. Morgan followed close behind, her dark hair whipping around her face as she navigated the maze-like shop.

Her mind raced, analyzing each turn and calculating the best route to corner Michael. Ten years in prison had honed her instincts, sharpened her senses, and she called upon every bit of that hard-earned experience now.

As Michael rounded a corner into a dead end, he realized his mistake too late. Derik was right behind him, grabbing hold of his arm and wrenching it back. The wrench clattered to the floor as Morgan joined them, breathing heavily but with a look of determination in her eyes.

"Got you," she panted, her gaze never leaving Michael's face. "Now let's talk."

"Fine!" Michael gasped, his chest heaving with exertion. "But I'm telling you, I don't know anything about those murders!"

Morgan took a moment to catch her breath. She needed answers, but could she trust this frightened man before her? One thing was certain: she wouldn't stop until the truth was uncovered.

With Michael secured and panting against the wall, Derik took out his cuffs and restrained him. Morgan glanced around the cluttered shop, her mind working furiously as she tried to piece together a connection between this man and the murders of Jennifer and Sarah.

"Derik, call for backup," she ordered, her voice steady despite the rapid beating of her heart. "We need to search this place thoroughly."

As they waited for their colleagues to arrive, Morgan and Derik began an impromptu search of the shop, rifling through drawers filled with mismatched keys and lockpicking tools. The air was thick with the metallic scent of keys and the dust that had accumulated over the years.

Morgan's thoughts raced as she sifted through the disarray, her instincts telling her that there was something amiss with Michael. But as she continued the search, she couldn't deny the nagging doubt that had taken root in her mind: did he truly fit the profile of the methodical killer they were seeking?

"Anything?" Derik asked, breaking the silence as he wiped the sweat from his brow.

"Nothing yet," Morgan admitted, frustration creeping into her voice. "But I can't shake the feeling that we're missing something."

"Maybe we are," Derik agreed. "Or maybe he's just not our guy."

The arrival of their backup team signaled the end of their impromptu search. Despite their best efforts, they found no evidence linking Michael to the murders. As the officers filed out of the shop, Morgan approached Michael, who was now sitting on the floor, his wrists still cuffed behind his back.

"Michael," she said, her tone softening slightly, "we didn't find anything here that connects you to the deaths of Jennifer or Sarah. But I need to know if you remember doing work for Jennifer all those years ago."

Michael looked up at her, his eyes wide and fearful. "I remember her," he said slowly. "And I know she died after I changed the locks on her place. But I swear, I didn't have anything to do with it."

"Sarah Benson was found dead too," Morgan informed him, watching for any change in his expression.

"Sarah?" Michael's voice cracked, genuine shock flashing across his face. "No, no, I didn't... I couldn't have..." His voice trailed off as he seemed to grapple with the revelation. Michael's face paled as he scrambled to explain his innocence, his voice shaking. "I-I can prove I wasn't here last night," he stammered. "I was in Dallas on a date with a woman I met through a dating app. It went terribly, and I ended up staying at a hotel there." He swallowed hard, desperation evident in his eyes. "I have receipts. You can check."

Morgan studied him for a moment, taking in the beads of sweat on his forehead and the way his fingers twitched nervously. Despite her doubts about his guilt, she couldn't ignore the fact that he had tried to run.

"Alright," Morgan said, her voice firm but not unkind. "We'll look into your alibi. But for now, you're under arrest for trying to avoid arrest and for suspicion of murder."

Michael's shoulders sagged, and he nodded, accepting his fate. Morgan signaled for the officers to take him away, watching as they escorted him out of the shop. She couldn't shake the nagging feeling that something was off - that Michael didn't fit the profile of the cold and calculating killer who had taken Jennifer and Sarah's lives.

And if that were the case, then they were nowhere closer to finding the killer.

CHAPTER SEVEN

The fluorescent lights in the Charlesberg police precinct's briefing room hummed a relentless symphony, casting an almost sickly hue over the worn tables and chairs. Morgan stood at the whiteboard, her dark hair pulled back into a tight ponytail, tattoos visible on her arms as she crossed them over her chest. The frustration on her face was palpable, mirrored by Derik, who sat across from her, green eyes bloodshot with fatigue.

"Damn it, Derik," Morgan muttered, clenching her jaw. "The locksmith had a solid alibi. He was in Dallas when Sarah was murdered. We're back to square one."

Derik rubbed his tired eyes and sighed, his slick black hair slightly disheveled. The strain of the case was taking its toll on both of them, but Derik's personal demons seemed to be weighing him down even more. Morgan knew he was fighting the constant battle against the bottle, just as she fought her own bitterness about her time in prison.

"Let's go over the other leads again," Derik suggested, leaning forward and rifling through the case files spread out on the table. "We can't have missed something."

Morgan stared at the whiteboard. She'd learned long ago to trust her instincts, honed by years of experience and sharpened by the injustice that had shaped her life. "I want to talk to some of Sarah's acquaintances myself," she said, feeling a spark of determination ignite within her. "The police conducted interviews, but maybe there's something they missed."

"Sounds like a plan," Derik agreed, closing the case file and straightening up. "Where do we start?"

"Sarah's cousin, Macy," Morgan replied, tapping her finger on the whiteboard next to the woman's name. "She was apparently close to Sarah. I want to know more about her life before she was murdered. It means driving back to Dallas, but it's worth a shot."

Derik nodded, his eyes meeting Morgan's with a mix of exhaustion and determination. They'd come a long way since he'd betrayed her trust, and despite everything, they were still partners - bound together by their shared pursuit of justice.

"Alright," Derik said, pushing back his chair and standing up. "Let's hit the road."

As they gathered their things and prepared to leave the precinct, Morgan couldn't shake the feeling that they were on the verge of a breakthrough. She didn't know what they would find in Dallas, but she knew she wouldn't rest until she brought Sarah's killer to justice.

***

The sun had already dipped below the horizon, casting a somber glow over the Dallas skyline as Morgan and Derik pulled up to Macy's apartment building. The air was heavy with humidity, the weight of it pressing down on them as they made their way up the concrete stairs to her door.

Morgan knocked, her knuckles rapping against the wood in a precise rhythm that echoed through the quiet hallway. Moments later, the door opened to reveal a young woman with red-rimmed eyes and a tear-streaked face. It was clear she'd been expecting them, but the sight of her grief still hit Morgan like a punch to the gut.

"Ms. Cross, Mr. Greene," Macy said, her voice wavering. "Please, come in."

"Thank you, Macy," Morgan replied softly, stepping into the warmth of the apartment. Derik followed close behind, his expression somber as he took in the surroundings.

The living room was cozy and welcoming, filled with well-worn furniture and personal trinkets that spoke of a life lived in earnest. It was a stark contrast to Sarah's eerily pristine house, where everything felt untouched and sterile. Here, there was a sense of familiarity and love that made the tragedy of Sarah's death all the more heart-wrenching.

Macy gestured for them to sit down on the plush sofa, sinking into an armchair across from them. "I-I'll answer any questions you have," she stammered, wiping fresh tears from her cheeks. "As long as it helps find whoever did this to Sarah."

"Thank you, Macy," Morgan said, her voice gentle but firm. "We appreciate your cooperation."

"Did Sarah ever mention anything unusual before she moved to Charlesberg?" Derik asked, leaning forward slightly.

Macy shook her head, her dark hair falling across her face as she tried to recall any pertinent details. "No, nothing like that," she said.

"She was excited about the new job, but... I think she was also a little scared to leave Dallas."

"Scared?" Morgan echoed, her brow furrowing as she considered this new information.

"Change is always scary," Derik mused, his green eyes distant, perhaps remembering his own struggles with change and the choices he'd made that had led him down a dark path.

With Macy's eyes glistening, Morgan leaned forward, her fingers laced together. "Why did Sarah move to Charlesberg?" she asked.

"Um," Macy sniffed, wiping her eyes with the back of her hand. "She got a new job there. A really good one, actually. She was hesitant at first because she loved living in Dallas so much." Her voice wavered as she spoke, but Morgan could see her determination to continue. "But the job paid well, and she'd even be able to afford a house instead of an apartment."

Morgan studied Macy's face, noticing the lines of exhaustion and sorrow etched into it. The decision to leave her beloved city had clearly been difficult for Sarah, but she ultimately chose to take that leap of faith. If only she had known what awaited her.

"Sarah's apartment here in Dallas," Macy continued, her voice trembling, "it's on the market now, but it hasn't sold yet. She moved away anyway, though. The job opportunity was time-sensitive, and she had to make a choice."

Macy's eyes welled up with tears again, her chin quivering as she fought to maintain her composure. "She didn't know that choice would be fatal."

Morgan felt a pang of sympathy for Macy, understanding the pain of losing someone dear to you. In her darkest days, locked away in prison, she had lost so many people who mattered to her. But she couldn't let her past cloud her focus.

"Thank you for sharing that, Macy," Morgan said quietly. "I know it's not easy to talk about."

Morgan and Derik exchanged a solemn glance. They both knew the importance of expressing their empathy but also pressing forward with their inquiry.

"Please know how truly sorry we are for your loss," Derik said, his voice tinged with a rare gentleness that Morgan hadn't often seen during their partnership. "We're doing everything we can to find the person responsible."

"Thank you," Macy replied, dabbing at her eyes with a crumpled tissue.

"Did Sarah have any enemies?" Morgan asked, studying Macy's face for any hint of hesitation. "Anyone who might hold a grudge against her?"

"None that I can think of," Macy answered, shaking her head. "Especially not in Charlesberg. She was just starting her life there."

"During the party you mentioned before," Morgan pressed on, "did you notice any strange men lurking around the house or appearing out of place?"

Macy's brow furrowed as she searched her memories. "No, I don't recall seeing anyone suspicious. I mean, everyone knew everyone. We'd notice if someone off was there."

As Morgan absorbed this information, she couldn't ignore the sinking feeling of another possible dead end. The trail was growing colder by the second, and the weight of her responsibility bore down on her like a thousand-ton anchor. She needed to solve this case, not only for Sarah and her family but for herself as well—to prove that she could overcome her past and make a difference in the present.

"Please be assured, Macy," Morgan said, her voice firm and determined, "we're doing our best to bring Sarah justice. We won't rest until her killer is caught."

"Thank you," Macy whispered, her voice tremulous but grateful. "That means more than you'll ever know."

In the silence that followed, Morgan's mind raced with thoughts and theories, desperately searching for any new connection or angle that had eluded her thus far. She could feel the pressure bearing down on her, threatening to suffocate her, but she refused to let it break her resolve.

I've faced tougher situations before, Morgan thought fiercely. *I won't let this case be my undoing. Sarah deserves justice, and I'm going to make damn sure she gets it.*

***

Back in the car, Morgan's fingers drummed impatiently on the steering wheel as Derik sifted through the case files spread across his lap. The hum of the engine and the distant sounds of the city were the only accompaniment to their silence, both lost in their own thoughts.

"Anything new from Macy's statement that stands out to you?" Morgan asked, her brows furrowed in concentration.

Derik shook his head, his green eyes scanning the pages intently. "Nothing that changes our current understanding. Just reaffirms Sarah had no known enemies."

"Let's go back to the locksmith angle," Morgan suggested, tapping a tattooed finger against her chin. "Maybe we missed something. And what about the unattended drink at the party? We need to look at all the angles, Derik."

"Right." He flipped back to the earlier notes. "No one saw anything suspicious around the drink, but there's always the chance they overlooked something. As for the locksmith, he was indeed in Dallas during the time of the murder."

"Has anyone checked if Sarah's apartment in Dallas had any changed locks or security updates recently?" Morgan asked, her dark hair falling into her face as she leaned forward with renewed interest.

Derik scanned the documents once more, then shook his head. "No information on that in the files. I can make a call and see if we can find something."

"Please do," Morgan said, frustration seeping into her voice. She gripped the steering wheel tighter, her knuckles whitening. It felt like they were hitting another wall, and she couldn't help but feel the weight of each dead end on her shoulders.

As Derik dialed the number, Morgan stared out the windshield, her mind racing with theories and connections. She knew they were close—that somewhere within the tangle of information, there was a thread waiting to be pulled, unraveling the truth behind Sarah's murder.

"Hey, it's Agent Greene," Derik said into his phone, drawing Morgan back to the present. "We're working on the Charlesberg case and need some information regarding Sarah's apartment in Dallas. Were there any recent changes to the locks or security updates? … Alright, thanks." He hung up and looked at Morgan with a resigned expression. "No changes to the locks or security updates in the last six months. It's another dead end."

"Dammit," Morgan muttered under her breath, her frustration reaching boiling point. She slumped back in her seat, knowing they needed a fresh perspective. But where would they find it? "I can't believe we're back to square one," she growled, her dark eyes smoldering with frustration.

"Hey," Derik said gently, his voice a calming presence amidst her storm of emotions. "We've been through worse, Morgan. Remember that last case in Dallas? We hit dead end after dead end, but we still solved it."

She shook her head, her arms crossed over her chest. "This feels different, Derik. We're so close, I can feel it. We just need something to tip us over the edge." She reached up and rubbed at the tension knotted between her brows. "A fresh perspective... but where do we find it?"

Derik leaned back in his seat, his eyes thoughtful as he stared at the ceiling. It was moments like these when he seemed older than his years, the weight of his past etched into the lines around his eyes. "Let's take a step back for a moment," he suggested. "Forget the locksmith connection and the unattended drink. What else do we know about Sarah's life? Maybe there's something we're overlooking."

Morgan sighed and rubbed her temples, an action mirrored by Derik as they both fell silent, lost in thought. After a few minutes, Morgan spoke up, her voice hesitant as if unsure of her own words. "What about her friends? Relationships? Did Macy mention anything about that?"

Derik frowned, recalling their conversation with Sarah's cousin. "Not much. Macy said Sarah had a good circle of friends here in Dallas, but nothing out of the ordinary. No recent breakups or arguments that she knew of."

"Maybe it's time we dig deeper into Sarah's personal life. There has to be something we're missing," Morgan mused, tapping her fingers on the steering wheel, her tattoos a blur of movement. "Even if it's just a small detail, it could be the key to unlocking this whole thing."

Derik nodded, his eyes regaining some of their earlier spark. "You're right. We'll figure this out, Morgan. We always do."

"Damn straight we will," she replied, the fire back in her voice. With renewed determination, they dove back into the case files and continued their search for the truth behind Sarah's murder.

CHAPTER EIGHT

The brisk autumn air nipped at the man's cheeks as he stood on the sidewalk, hands in his pockets, surveying the bustling open house of a downtown apartment complex. The throng of potential homebuyers buzzed around him, their laughter and excited chatter filling the crisp afternoon. He appeared to be just another face in the crowd, casually observing the tall building before him.

"Nice place, isn't it?" A voice emerged from behind him, causing him to turn. A real estate agent, dressed impeccably in a navy-blue suit, extended a hand. "I'm Tim Bannon, one of the agents showing these units."

"Ah, yes," the man replied, shaking Tim's hand firmly. "It's quite impressive. I'm looking for a nice, secure place to settle down in the city."

"Security is definitely a priority here," Tim assured him, gesturing towards the building. "Each unit has its own state-of-the-art security system, and all the locks have been recently updated."

He smiled. Was that so?

As they stepped inside, the man's eyes flickered across each apartment's door, mentally cataloging every lock and potential vulnerability. To him, these barriers were not meant to keep people out; rather, they were intriguing puzzles waiting to be solved. His heart raced with anticipation, his fingers itching to caress the cold metal and deftly maneuver hidden pins until they yielded to his touch.

"You mentioned that the locks were changed recently," the man said, feigning casual interest. "Any particular reason for that?"

"Mostly just routine maintenance," Tim replied, leading him through the crowded hallway.

"Interesting," the man mused, an unsettling glint in his eye. "You can never be too careful these days, can you?"

"Absolutely," Tim agreed, not picking up on the man's hidden intentions. "Let me show you one of the available units, and we can discuss further security features."

As they continued their tour, the man couldn't help but revel in the twisted thrill that coursed through him. He was a predator among unsuspecting prey, his true intentions masked by a veneer of polite interest. And with every lock he observed, every question he asked, he felt himself drawing closer to his next exhilarating challenge.

Amidst the lively chatter of potential buyers and the hum of anticipation, he spotted her. Lucy. She was a radiant figure in the crowded room, her laughter effervescent like champagne bubbles. Her body swayed gracefully as she conversed with others, a testament to her profession as a dancer. He could sense her vibrant energy even from across the room as she inspected the spacious living area with its expansive windows revealing the cityscape below.

"Excuse me," the man said, cutting short his conversation with Tim. "I need a moment." The real estate agent nodded, his attention diverted by other inquisitive visitors. It was all too easy for the man to slip away, weaving through the crowd while keeping Lucy in his peripheral vision.

"Isn't this place just amazing?" Lucy exclaimed to a young couple nearby, her eyes sparkling with excitement. "I just moved into this building, but I just had to see this unit too! I can totally picture my dance routines in this open space!"

As she spoke, the man's anticipation built, his mind racing with detailed plans and cold calculations. He stood there among the throng of people, his presence unnoticed and calm – an unassuming shadow waiting for the perfect moment to strike.

***

The dim glow of a single desk lamp illuminated the otherwise dark room, casting long shadows across the cluttered surface. Blueprints and architectural schematics lay scattered about, interspersed with an assortment of lockpicking tools that gleamed menacingly in the limited light. The air was heavy, suffocating—laden with a palpable sense of malice.

"Ah, home sweet home," the man murmured to himself, his voice devoid of warmth as he surveyed the confined space. He deftly removed the stolen master key from his pocket, allowing it to dangle before his eyes like a tantalizing prize. "Now, let's see if you're everything I hoped for."

He approached a small workbench, where a lock identical to those found at the apartment complex had been mounted. With practiced ease, he inserted the master key into the keyhole, turning it slowly. A soft click resounded through the silent room, sending a shiver down his spine—a twisted form of satisfaction that only such a game could provide.

"Perfect," he whispered, withdrawing the key and setting it aside. He'd made it himself, and he was a master at it. His fingers danced over the array of lockpicking tools, each one a testament to his macabre obsession. Selecting a tension wrench and pick, he set to work on the lock once more, his movements fluid and precise.

"Lucy," he mused, her name rolling off his tongue like a forbidden secret. "Such a lovely girl. So full of life and passion... It's a shame, really."

His thoughts drifted to the vibrant dancer he'd observed earlier, her every move etched into his memory. She was the embodiment of all that he desired—innocent, yet fierce. Her presence had ignited something within him, fueling his anticipation for their inevitable encounter.

"Every lock has its secrets," he muttered, feeling the tumbler pins give way beneath his expert touch. "Just like people. And unlocking them... that's the true art."

The lock clicked open once more, and he allowed himself a small, sinister grin. To him, this was not an act of criminality, but rather a challenge—an intricate dance between predator and prey.

"Lucy, my dear," he said softly, his cold eyes reflecting the dim light in the room. "I hope you're ready for our little game. I've been waiting for someone like you."

With each meticulous detail of his plan laid out before him, the man reveled in the thrill of the hunt.

Soon.

Lucy would meet her end soon.

No lock could keep him out.

CHAPTER NINE

Morgan gripped the steering wheel tightly, her knuckles turning white as she navigated the midday traffic on their way back to Charlesberg. The sun beat down on the windshield, casting a harsh light on her frustration. Normally, by this point in an investigation, she and Derik would have made significant progress, but this case seemed to defy them at every turn.

In the passenger seat, Derik rifled through files with a quiet intensity, scanning pages for any detail they might have missed. Morgan couldn't help but notice how tired he looked, the shadows under his eyes betraying the toll his personal life took on him. She knew better than anyone that trust could be fragile, and although she had started to forgive him for his past betrayal, it still hung between them like a specter.

"Hey, Morgan," Derik said, breaking the silence. "Did you know that Jennifer's house never sold again after her murder?"

Morgan glanced over at him, her dark brows furrowing. "No, I didn't. Why not?"

"Apparently, it's been condemned due to black mold," he continued, lifting a page from the file to show her. "No one ever bought it or bothered to clean up the place."

"Sounds like a lovely spot for a field trip," Morgan replied. The thought of stepping foot in such a place made her skin crawl, but she couldn't deny the nagging feeling that there might be something crucial hidden within its decaying walls. "Let's head there," she decided, making a sharp turn onto the exit ramp that would lead them towards the condemned house.

Eventually, the car rolled to a stop in front of the house, its boarded-up windows and overgrown yard a stark contrast to the manicured lawns and pristine facades of the neighboring homes. Morgan felt a chill run down her spine as she took in the scene, a grim reminder that even the most idyllic neighborhoods could harbor dark secrets.

"Here goes nothing," she muttered under her breath, forcing herself to step out of the car and onto the cracked pavement. Derik followed suit, his eyes scanning the area for any signs of life or danger.

As they stood there, an elderly woman emerged from the house next door, a small dog on a leash trotting beside her. She looked at them curiously, her kind eyes filled with both wariness and concern. Morgan took the opportunity to approach her, hoping she might have some information about the ill-fated Jennifer.

"Excuse me," Morgan said, her voice gentle but firm. "Did you know the person who lived here?"

The woman's face paled, and she clutched her dog's leash tightly. "Yes," she replied, swallowing hard. "I remember Jennifer. She only lived here for a short time before... it happened." The word 'it' hung heavy in the air, charged with emotion and unspoken horrors. Morgan nodded solemnly, understanding exactly what the woman meant.

"Can you tell me why no one ever bought this house and cleared the black mold?" Morgan asked, her gaze shifting back to the dilapidated building. "It seems like a waste of space in such a nice neighborhood."

The old woman glanced at the house, her expression darkening. "There's a big superstitious community here in Charlesberg, dear," she explained. "Many people think the house is haunted." She shuddered slightly, as if the mere thought of ghosts unsettled her.

Morgan suppressed an eye roll. As far as she was concerned, there were no such things as ghosts. The only monsters lurking in the shadows were the living – the murderers, the rapists, the thieves. They were the ones who truly haunted the world, not some imaginary spirits.

"Thank you for your help," Morgan told the woman sincerely before turning to Derik. "Let's check out the house."

Together, they approached the sad-looking structure, its wooden boards covered in graffiti and grime. Morgan took a deep breath, steeling herself for what they might discover inside, and then kicked in the door with a powerful swing of her leg. It splintered open, revealing the dark interior tainted by decay and neglect.

As soon as they stepped inside, the stench of mold and dampness assaulted their nostrils. Morgan and Derik both pulled their shirts up over their noses, trying to shield themselves from the harmful spores that undoubtedly filled the air.

"God, this place is a mess," Derik commented, his voice muffled by the fabric of his shirt. "Why didn't anyone take care of it?"

"Superstition," Morgan reminded him, her mind returning to the neighbor's words. "People believe this place is cursed or something."

She shook her head, frustrated by the irrationality of it all. If someone had just taken the time to clean up the place, maybe they would have discovered something – a clue, a hint, anything that could help them solve Jennifer's murder and bring her killer to justice. But instead, the house had been left to rot, forgotten by everyone except the ghosts that supposedly haunted its halls.

"Let's see what we can find," Morgan said, determination filling her voice. "We won't let this place scare us away."

And with that, she stepped further into the darkness, ready to confront whatever secrets the house might hold.

The scent of decay grew stronger as they ventured further into the house, their shoes crunching on broken glass and debris. As they entered the living room, Morgan's breath caught in her throat. The remnants of Jennifer's life clung to the walls like a sickly residue – dried blood spatters, streaks of gore – a testament to the violence that had taken place here.

"Jesus," Derik murmured, his eyes wide as he took in the gruesome scene. "No wonder people think this place is haunted."

Morgan clenched her fists, anger rising within her. "This isn't about ghosts, Derik. This is about a human being who was murdered, and whoever did it didn't even have the decency to clean up after themselves."

"Sorry," Derik said quickly, realizing his misstep. "You're right. Let's focus on what we came here for."

They began searching the room, careful not to disturb the fragile crime scene any further. Morgan's gaze lingered on the locks of the doors, which appeared to be the same type as those found at Sarah's house. She frowned, remembering how they'd already cleared the locksmith.

"Derik, come look at this," she called to him, pointing at the lock. "Doesn't this look familiar?"

"Damn," he replied, examining the lock more closely. "It's identical to the one on Sarah's door. But we already cleared Michael Rivers, so who else could it be?"

Morgan chewed on her lip, deep in thought. "I don't know, but there has to be some sort of connection. We can't ignore this."

"Agreed," Derik nodded. "We'll keep digging. Maybe there's someone else out there who knows about these locks."

As they continued their search, Morgan couldn't shake the feeling that they were on the cusp of a breakthrough. The untampered locks seemed to be the key – no pun intended – to unlocking the truth behind Jennifer and Sarah's murders.

"Whoever did this has a sick sense of humor, leaving their signature right in front of our noses," she muttered under her breath. "But we'll find them. We have to."

With renewed determination, Morgan pressed on, sifting through the remnants of Jennifer's life, hoping that somewhere among the debris, they would find the answers they were seeking.

Morgan stepped into the kitchen, her eyes widening at the sight before her. The room was a time capsule, remnants of Jennifer's life left undisturbed for years. Dust-covered dishes sat in the sink, long-forgotten letters cluttered the counters, and paperwork was strewn about the table. It sent a shiver down her spine – it felt like walking into a ghost's home, a chilling reminder of the horrors that had taken place within these walls.

"Derik," Morgan said, her voice barely above a whisper as she took in the scene. "Look at all this."

"Jesus," he muttered, his green eyes scanning the room. "It's like she just... vanished. Like everyone just forgot about her."

"Or didn't care enough to clean up after her," Morgan added bitterly, the anger resurfacing at the thought of Jennifer's tragic end being reduced to a mere urban legend.

She began sifting through the documents on the table, her fingers brushing against yellowed envelopes and curling post-it notes. One particular document caught her eye – a house sale agreement, detailing Jennifer's old apartment being put up for sale. Morgan furrowed her brow, feeling a strange connection between the two cases now staring back at her.

"Hey, Derik," she called out, motioning him over. "Take a look at this."

"House sale document?" he asked, leaning in to examine the paperwork. After a moment, he nodded. "Seems legit. I guess she was selling her old apartment to move in here."

"Right," Morgan replied. "So, she moved from one place to another, just like Sarah. There has to be something more to this – we need to find out more about Jennifer's life. We should seek out her family."

"Agreed," Derik responded, his tired eyes meeting hers. "We're onto something here, Morgan. I can feel it."

"Me too," she said, determination creeping back into her voice as they prepared to delve deeper into the mystery that had haunted Charlesberg for far too long.

CHAPTER TEN

The drive out to the old age home was a contemplative one, with Morgan's thoughts drifting back and forth between Jennifer and Sarah. As they pulled into the parking lot of the sprawling nursing home, Derik turned to her, his green eyes clouded with concern.

"Hey, what are you hoping to find here?" he asked gently. "I mean, I know we need more information on Jennifer, but what do you think will help us crack this case?"

Morgan stared at the quaint, well-kept buildings for a moment before answering. "I'm not sure," she admitted, her voice low and tentative. "But something tells me that Jennifer's murder is the key to solving Sarah's. We have to explore every angle."

Derik nodded, his expression resolute. "Alright then. Let's see what we can dig up."

They got out of the car and made their way to the main office, passing by residents chatting amiably in the courtyard or enjoying leisurely strolls along the manicured paths. The peaceful atmosphere of the nursing home seemed in stark contrast to the darkness of the case they were investigating. Morgan couldn't help but wonder if she would ever find herself in such a place, her tattoos hidden beneath long sleeves and her past buried deep within her heart.

As they entered the main office, the faint scent of fresh flowers filled the air, and Morgan felt an odd mix of comfort and unease. They approached the reception desk, where a cheerful woman greeted them with a warm smile. Morgan felt the weight of her FBI badge in her hand as she presented it to the receptionist. The fluorescent lights above cast a sterile glow over them, highlighting the contrast between Morgan's tattoos and Derik's tailored suit.

"Special Agent Morgan Cross, and this is my partner, Special Agent Derik Greene," she said with a firm tone. "We're looking for a resident named Sharol Stacy."

"Ah, yes, Ms. Stacy," the receptionist replied, her voice softening with understanding. "She's in her room right now. I'll take you there."

They followed the receptionist down the carpeted corridor, their footsteps muffled by the plush fabric beneath them. Morgan couldn't help but notice how each room seemed to be a small world unto itself, filled with personal belongings and memories. It was a far cry from the cold, institutional spaces she had known in her past.

As they approached Sharol Stacy's room, the receptionist hesitated for a moment before turning to face them. Her previous cheerfulness gave way to concern. "I just need to warn you, Ms. Stacy is... well, she's been through a lot. We try our best to keep her life as stress-free as possible."

Morgan glanced at Derik, who nodded solemnly. She knew they were treading on sensitive ground, but they couldn't afford to leave any stone unturned. "We understand," she assured the receptionist. "We're here to talk about her daughter, Jennifer. We believe it may help us with an ongoing investigation."

The receptionist's eyes widened with comprehension, and she gave a slow nod. "I see. All right then." She rapped gently on the door, the sound echoing through the hallway like a harbinger of the delicate conversation to come.

"Ms. Stacy?" the receptionist called softly, her voice laced with caution. "There are some people here from the FBI who'd like to speak with you about Jennifer."

Morgan's heart raced as they waited for a response, already working through potential scenarios and responses. She knew that every answer, every word exchanged, could be the key to unlocking the truth – and she was determined not to let it slip through her fingers.

"Come in," came the shaky voice from within the room.

Morgan exchanged a glance with Derik before pushing open the door, her heart pounding in anticipation. As they entered, they were greeted by an elderly woman in a wheelchair, her gaze fixed on the sunlit gardens outside her window. The receptionist offered them a tight-lipped smile before slipping back out into the hallway, leaving them alone with Ms. Stacy.

"Ms. Stacy?" Morgan inquired gently, approaching the older woman with caution. "We're Agents Morgan Cross and Derik Greene from the FBI. We'd like to talk to you about your daughter, Jennifer, if that's all right."

The tension in the room was palpable as Ms. Stacy's eyes flickered away from the vibrant colors of the garden and met Morgan's, her face drawn with both curiosity and trepidation. "What about Jennifer?" she asked, her voice wavering.

"Another young woman was recently found dead in Charlesberg," Morgan explained, trying to keep her tone as steady and reassuring as possible. "There are... similarities between her case and Jennifer's."

"Similarities?" The word seemed to catch in Ms. Stacy's throat, her knuckles turning white as she gripped the armrests of her wheelchair. Despite the wrinkles etched deep into her skin and the pain clouding her gaze, there was a fierce determination in her eyes – the same kind of determination that had driven Morgan throughout her own darkest hours.

"We believe there may be a connection between the two cases," Derik interjected, his voice quiet but firm. "And we think that by looking more closely at Jennifer's murder, we might be able to find answers for both victims."

Ms. Stacy stared at them for a long moment, her face a mosaic of conflicting emotions. Then, with a slow nod, she turned her wheelchair to face them fully, her hands trembling ever so slightly. "All right," she said, at last, her voice barely audible. "I'll help you any way I can."

As Morgan looked into Ms. Stacy's eyes – old and wise, yet brimming with sorrow – she was reminded of just how high the stakes were in this investigation. They weren't simply seeking justice for one victim; they were fighting for two families who had been shattered by unthinkable tragedy. And as she prepared to delve into the painful memories that would inevitably arise, she vowed to do everything in her power to ensure their suffering would not be in vain.

"Can you tell us anything about Jennifer's life leading up to her death?" Morgan asked, her voice gentle but determined. "We know she had moved into a new house not long before she was killed and that she was in the process of selling her old apartment."

Sharol's eyes filled with tears as she recalled her daughter's enthusiasm for the new chapter in her life. "Jennifer was so excited about that house," she began, her voice wavering. "She couldn't stop talking about how it was going to be the perfect place to start a family." Sharol paused, swallowing hard, as if the words were lodged in her throat. "She had just gotten engaged, you see. They were planning their future together."

Morgan watched as Sharol fought to maintain her composure, her heart aching for the older woman. In those moments, it was all too easy to remember the pain of her own mother's loss – the heavy burden of grief that had weighed on her soul like a millstone.

As the conversation continued, Derik stepped in, sensing that delving deeper into these memories was taking a toll on Sharol. He asked her about any unusual events or incidents that might have occurred around the time Jennifer moved into her new home.

Sharol hesitated for a moment, her brow furrowing as she searched her memory. Then, she gave a small nod, her expression somber. "There was something," she said quietly. "Not long before she was killed, Jennifer told me that her old apartment had been broken into. But the odd thing was, nothing seemed to be stolen."

Morgan's attention sharpened at this revelation. It was an unexpected lead, one that could potentially shed light on the killer's motives and methods. She remained quiet, allowing Derik to ask the necessary follow-up questions while she absorbed the information.

"Did the police investigate the break-in?" Derik asked, his green eyes fixed on Sharol's face.

"Jennifer filed a report, but the police didn't seem to take it very seriously," Sharol admitted, her voice tinged with bitterness. "They said there was no sign of forced entry, and since nothing was taken, they brushed it off as a false alarm."

But something in Morgan's gut told her that Jennifer's break-in was far from an isolated incident – that it might, in fact, be a crucial piece of the puzzle that had eluded them until now. As she watched Sharol struggle with the weight of her memories, she vowed to uncover the truth, no matter what it took.

Sharol's hands trembled as she carried on with her story, the memories of Jennifer's ordeal resurfacing like a painful wound. "Jennifer was so scared after that break-in," she said, her voice barely audible. "She told me that even though nothing was taken, some things in her apartment had been moved around... as if someone had been rifling through her belongings."

Morgan leaned forward, her dark eyes narrowed in concentration. "Did Jennifer ever mention feeling like she was being followed or watched?"

Sharol hesitated for a moment, then nodded. "Yes, she did. She couldn't shake the feeling that someone was always lurking in the shadows, watching her every move." Her voice broke as she added, "I tried to reassure her, telling her it was just her imagination running wild, but I should have listened to her. I should have believed her..."

"Sharol, you couldn't have known what would happen," Morgan said softly, her own heart aching for the grieving mother.

"Did Jennifer ever report this feeling of being followed to the police?" Derik asked gently.

"Jennifer mentioned it in passing when she filed the break-in report, but again, they didn't take her seriously," Sharol replied, the frustration evident in her voice. "The police insisted that since the locks were untouched, it must have been a figment of her imagination. But Jennifer wasn't one to make up stories, and she was always so cautious about locking up her apartment."

As Morgan listened to Sharol's words, her thoughts raced with the implications. Was it possible that the person who had broken into Jennifer's old apartment was the same person who had murdered her in her new home? And if so, what was their connection to Sarah's case?

"Sharol, do you know if Jennifer ever suspected anyone in particular?" Morgan asked, hoping for a lead.

"No, she didn't," Sharol replied, shaking her head. "But she always had this nagging feeling that someone had it out for her. She just couldn't put her finger on who or why."

"Thank you, Sharol," Morgan said, her voice firm with determination. "You've given us valuable information to work with. We'll do everything we can to uncover the truth and bring Jennifer's killer to justice."

As Morgan and Derik left the nursing home, Morgan's mind churned with possibilities. The connection between Jennifer and Sarah's cases seemed to hinge on those seemingly innocuous locks. But with the locksmith already cleared, who else could have tampered with them, leaving no trace behind? And what did it mean for their ongoing investigation?

CHAPTER ELEVEN

Morgan's fingers drummed on the steering wheel as she drove back to the precinct, her mind preoccupied with the locks. If Michael Rivers was truly innocent, then who else could have tampered with them? The unsettling thought gnawed at her, like a persistent itch she couldn't quite reach. Beside her, Derik stared out the window, lost in his thoughts.

"Whoever this person is, they know their way around locks," Morgan muttered, more to herself than to anyone else. "And they're careful. Very careful."

"True," Derik agreed, his gaze still focused on the passing scenery. "But if it's not Rivers, then who?"

Morgan shook her head, frustrated. "I don't know. But there's got to be something we're missing."

A heavy silence settled in the car, broken only by the hum of the engine and the faint sound of traffic outside.

Back at the precinct, Morgan strode into the bullpen with renewed determination, Derik trailing behind her. They might be at a dead end, but she refused to let that stop her. There had to be a clue somewhere, hidden just beneath the surface.

"Alright," she said, dropping into her chair and opening her laptop. "Let's go over everything again. Maybe we missed something."

"Another round?" Derik asked, his voice laced with exhaustion. He rubbed his eyes and sighed. "Alright. Let's do it."

As they reviewed the case files, Morgan couldn't shake the feeling that the key to solving Sarah's murder lay in Jennifer's past. That break-in at her old apartment...it wasn't normal. It was a sign that someone had been stalking her, watching her every move before striking. And if that was the case, then perhaps Sarah had been stalked as well.

"Derik," she said, her voice low and urgent. "I think we need to look more closely at everyone who knew both victims. If we can find someone with a motive and the skills to pull off these murders..."

"Then we might have our killer," Derik finished, his eyes lighting up with understanding.

"Exactly," Morgan replied, her determination growing stronger with each passing moment. "So let's get to work. I don't want to waste another second."

As they dove back into their investigation, Morgan felt that they were on the verge of a breakthrough. And when it came, she would be ready.

Morgan's fingertips drummed on the cold metal of her desk, her gaze fixed on the array of case files before her. The precinct buzzed with background noise as officers hurried past, their footsteps echoing on the linoleum floor. But all she could focus on was the nagging feeling that they were missing something crucial.

"Derik," she said, her voice laced with determination. "I know we cleared Michael Rivers, but there has to be someone else who could tamper with those locks."

Derik leaned back in his chair and rubbed his weary green eyes. "You think we're dealing with a lock-picking expert?" He asked, skepticism etching lines into his tired face.

"Maybe," Morgan replied, her dark brows furrowing in thought. "But if they're not a professional locksmith, then they must have learned their skills somewhere else...like the criminal world."

A spark ignited behind Derik's eyes as he sat up straighter. "You're suggesting we look for known thieves in the area? Ones skilled enough to pick those locks without leaving a trace?"

"Exactly." Morgan stood up, her muscles tense with purpose, and strode over to the filing cabinet in the corner of the room. She yanked open the drawer labeled "Burglaries" and pulled out several folders, scattering them across her desk.

"Help me sort through these," she instructed Derik, her tone urgent. "We need to find anyone with a history of lockpicking."

As they flipped through pages of reports and mugshots, Morgan couldn't help but feel the weight of the victims' lives pressing down on her. She knew that for every moment they spent searching, the killer remained at large, free to stalk and murder again.

Morgan's fingers trembled slightly as she leafed through the stack of files, her eyes scanning each page for any hint of a connection. The smell of stale coffee and sweat hung in the air, a tangible reminder of the long hours they'd spent poring over case after case.

"Arthur McTavish," she whispered, the name catching her eye like a beacon in the darkness. She read on, taking in every detail of the nimble-fingered thief's criminal history. "Derik, look at this."

"Who's that?" Derik asked, his voice low and tired as he leaned over to see the file Morgan held.

"Arthur McTavish. He's known for his lockpicking skills," she explained, her voice barely more than a breath. "And he just got out of prison. He's back on the streets."

"Interesting," Derik mused, rubbing at his weary eyes. "Could he be our guy?"

"Maybe." Morgan hesitated, her chest tightening with uncertainty. She knew that pinning their hopes on a single suspect was always risky, especially when there was so much at stake. But something about McTavish's record spoke to her, a whisper of intuition that she couldn't ignore. "His rap sheet is full of minor offenses, mostly breaking and entering, theft, possession of burglary tools. But what sets him apart is his expertise in lockpicking."

"Sounds like he could be worth checking out," Derik agreed, nodding slowly. "Do you think it's possible he picked up some new tricks while he was in prison? Maybe learned how to kill without leaving a trace?"

"Could be," Morgan said, her pulse quickening at the thought. "But we won't know for sure until we get eyes on him."

"Alright, let's track him down." Derik's voice took on a new determination, the weariness momentarily pushed aside. "If he's as good as his reputation suggests, we need to find him before he disappears again."

"Agreed," Morgan replied, clutching the file tightly as they turned their attention back to the task at hand. As they delved deeper into McTavish's criminal past, she felt that they were finally on the right track. And if her instincts were correct, it was only a matter of time before they found the monster responsible for Jennifer and Sarah's deaths.

But with each passing moment, Morgan knew the stakes grew higher. For all they knew, Arthur McTavish could be stalking his next victim even now, slipping through the night like a shadow. She steeled herself, vowing not to rest until the killer was caught—or until she had exhausted every last possibility.

***

Morgan and Derik strode purposefully toward the unassuming bar on a quiet Charlesberg street. The sun was still low in the sky, casting long shadows that stretched out before them. Despite the early hour, the bar's neon sign hummed to life, an indicator of the establishment's readiness for patrons.

"Word from the locals is that McTavish has been coming here since he got out," Morgan said, her dark eyes scanning the bar's facade, noting the peeling paint and smudged windows.

Derik nodded, his green eyes betraying a hint of fatigue despite his professional attire. "Let's hope we find him here."

As they entered the dimly lit bar, the scent of stale alcohol and lingering cigarette smoke greeted them. Eyes adjusting to the change in light, they scanned the room, taking in the few patrons who had already begun their day with a drink. The bar exuded a quiet elegance, a relic of times gone by, when Charlesberg had been a thriving town. Now, it was reduced to a haven for those seeking solace at the bottom of a bottle.

"Seems like even a town like Charlesberg isn't immune to its share of drunks," Derik commented, his voice tinged with empathy as he recalled his own struggles with addiction.

"Let's focus on finding McTavish," Morgan replied, her tone curt but not unkind. She knew too well the pain that haunted her partner; it was a shared burden they carried in their quest for redemption.

As they surveyed the bar, Morgan's thoughts turned to Arthur McTavish, the infamous ex-con known for his lockpicking skills. An unlikely lead, perhaps, but one worth pursuing given the recent string of murders. The victims' homes had been seemingly locked from the inside, their security systems untouched. It was a puzzle that had left the authorities stumped.

"Let's split up," Morgan suggested, her eyes narrowing as she scanned the faces of the bar patrons. "We're looking for a man with a distinct scar. I'll take the left side; you take the right."

"Got it," Derik replied, his gaze already focused on his designated area.

They moved silently through the room, their senses attuned to any sign of the man they sought. Morgan's thoughts were a whirlwind of determination and doubt. Was McTavish the key to unlocking this case? Or was he just another dead end in an investigation that seemed to be going nowhere?

She couldn't shake the feeling that something was amiss. Their partnership, once a seamless dance of intuition and trust, had been fractured by betrayal and loss. Now, they stood at a precipice, the weight of their past threatening to consume them. But there was no time for doubts, not when lives hung in the balance.

"Over here," Derik whispered, his voice barely audible above the low hum of conversation and clinking glasses. He gestured toward a solitary figure nursing a pint at the back of the bar.

Morgan joined him, her gaze fixed on the man with the unmistakable scar. This was it. They had found Arthur McTavish.

"Stay sharp, Derik," she cautioned, steeling herself for the confrontation ahead. "We don't know what we're walking into."

Morgan's eyes flickered across the dimly lit bar, momentarily lingering on the scar etched into the flesh beneath Arthur McTavish's left eye. The crude line marred an otherwise handsome face, a constant reminder of his criminal past. She exchanged a brief nod with Derik and moved toward their target, her steps steady and purposeful.

"Arthur McTavish?" she asked, her voice measured but firm. The man glanced up from his beer, his gray eyes meeting hers with a mixture of curiosity and wariness.

"Who's asking?" he replied, his raspy voice laced with suspicion.

Morgan revealed her FBI badge, as did Derik. "I'm Special Agent Morgan Cross, and this is my partner, Special Agent Derik Greene," she introduced. "We have some questions for you."

Arthur studied them for a moment before sighing heavily and gesturing for them to sit. "Fine. But I ain't making any promises about answering."

As they took their seats, Morgan couldn't help but feel the weight of her father's legacy bearing down on her. Christopher Cross, the man who had taught her how to read people, how to see through their lies, was now a ghost of a memory—a memory that seemed to haunt her every move.

"What do you want to know?" Arthur asked, interrupting her thoughts.

"Let's start with what you've been doing since your release from prison," Morgan said, her gaze never leaving his scarred visage. "Have you picked any locks recently?"

Arthur's response came in the form of a dry chuckle. "You think I'd be sitting here if I was still in that line of work? No, Agent Cross, I'm done with that life."

"Really?" she pressed, her instincts telling her there was more to his story. "And why is that?"

"Three years behind bars changes a man," Arthur replied, his voice taking on a somber tone. "I've got a daughter I'm not allowed to see. It's time for me to change my ways."

Morgan studied him. The faint light filtering through the bar's dusty windows cast an eerie glow on Arthur's face as he sat hunched over his drink. Morgan couldn't help but notice the way he held himself, the air of dignity that seemed to radiate from him despite the grime and despair of his surroundings. It was a curiosity, she thought, for a man with a criminal past.

“You sure you haven’t picked any locks recently?” she asked.

Arthur laughed, a hollow, bitter sound that echoed through the near-empty bar. He locked eyes with Morgan, the intensity of his gaze unwavering. "I'm done with that life, Agent Cross. Whatever it is you want, I can't help you."

Morgan studied him for a moment. She took a deep breath and pushed forward. "Why the sudden change of heart, then? Why abandon the criminal life now?"

Arthur's eyes grew distant, and shadows flickered across his face as he hesitated. Finally, he spoke, his voice tinged with regret. "This last time I was inside, it cost me more than just my freedom. My ex-girlfriend had a baby while I was away, and I'm not allowed to see them. I want to change, to be better."

As he spoke, Morgan felt a twinge of empathy stir within her, unbidden and unwanted. She knew the pain of losing someone, the weight of guilt and betrayal that could suffocate even the strongest among them. But she couldn't afford to let her guard down, not now. So instead, she pressed her lips into a thin line and focused on the task at hand, her inner turmoil tucked safely behind her steely gaze.

"Arthur, we're investigating a series of crimes where the locks were left seemingly untouched," she said, her voice even and unyielding. "We need to know if you have any information that might help us."

"Look," Arthur replied, a note of frustration creeping into his tone. "I don't know anything about that. I just want to be left alone, okay? I'm trying to put my life back together."

Derik cleared his throat, drawing Morgan's attention back to the dimly lit bar. "Arthur," he began, his voice measured and calm. "Have you heard about the death of a new Charlesberg resident named Sarah Benson?"

Arthur shook his head, looking genuinely perplexed. "No idea. I've been avoiding the news lately. Mostly just sitting here and drinking."

Morgan glanced around at the empty glasses on the table, her gaze sharp and critical. "Not doing much to change your ways if you're just a drunk," she remarked, raising an eyebrow.

"Mind your business," Arthur snapped, his tone acidic. "I'm working on myself in the best way I can."

Morgan bit back a retort and refocused her efforts on their investigation. "You may have left that life behind, but we need to know about your lock-picking skills." She studied him intently, gauging his reaction.

Arthur straightened in his chair, a glint of pride in his eyes. "It's true that I'm an expert at picking locks," he said, as if it were a badge of honor. "And I'm proud of it."

Morgan frowned, her thoughts racing as she tried to reconcile his words with the facts of their case. The precision and subtlety displayed at the crime scenes didn't match Arthur's boastful admission, conflicting with her profile of the killer. But she couldn't dismiss him outright; there was still too much they didn't know.

"Your expertise might be useful to us in this case," she said cautiously, the wheels in her mind turning relentlessly. "If you truly want to change, maybe you could help us catch a dangerous criminal."

Arthur didn't reply, simply gave them the cold shoulder, so Morgan decided to test her luck with him a bit more.

"Alright, Arthur," Morgan said, her voice steely and resolute. "Let's put those skills to the test."

She reached into her pocket and pulled out an evidence bag, holding it up for him to see. Inside was a replica of the locks used at both Jennifer and Sarah's houses. The sight of it seemed to rattle Arthur, his eyes narrowing as he regarded her with suspicion.

"Show us how you'd pick this lock," she demanded, her gaze unwavering.

"Are you out of your mind?" Arthur spat, his voice rising in anger. "You want me to incriminate myself right here, in front of everyone? I told you, I'm done with that life."

The commotion caught the attention of the few bar patrons lingering around, their bleary gazes turning toward the unfolding confrontation. Derik shifted uncomfortably beside Morgan, aware of the potential dangers of pursuing unverified suspects.

"Arthur, we just want to understand how it could have been done," Morgan pressed on, her voice softer but no less determined. "We're trying to catch a killer, someone who's using the same skills you possess. Your help could save lives."

"Enough!" Arthur bellowed, slamming his fist down on the table. "I've got nothing to do with this, and I won't be dragged back into that world!"

As the bar patrons began to murmur and move closer, curiosity piqued by the scene unfolding before them, Arthur seized the opportunity to slip away. He pushed past the gathering crowd and made a beeline for the exit, disappearing from sight.

"Damn it!" Morgan muttered under her breath, frustration mounting as she watched their suspect vanish. She turned to see the agitated faces of the bar patrons closing in, demanding answers.

"Everybody, please calm down," Derik spoke up, raising his hands in a placating gesture. "We're federal agents investigating a case, and we apologize for the disturbance. There's no need to worry; everything is under control."

His calm demeanor and steady voice seemed to have the desired effect, as the patrons slowly backed away, their curiosity sated for the moment. With a shared look of understanding, Morgan and Derik made their way out of the bar, the weight of another lead gone cold pressing down on them.

A gust of wind whipped at Morgan's face as she stepped out onto the sidewalk. She glanced up and down the street, searching for Arthur. Derik followed close behind her, both of them on high alert.

"Where did he go?" Derik asked, his voice tense.

"Over there!" Morgan pointed to a figure in the distance, leisurely strolling away from the bar. Though he seemed unaware that they had emerged from the establishment, his nonchalance struck her as odd.

"Hey! Arthur!" Morgan shouted, breaking into a run and closing the distance between them. To her surprise, he stopped and turned around, his expression unreadable.

"Look, I already told you, I can't help you," Arthur said, his voice cold and hard. "I'm not getting involved in whatever mess you're investigating."

"Listen," Morgan panted, catching her breath. "We're looking for someone who's an expert at leaving locks completely untouched—like a building locked from the inside with no signs of tampering."

Arthur's eyes narrowed, studying her carefully. "And you think I'm your guy? Like I said, I'm staying clean. I don't want any part of this."

Derik caught up to them, adding, "Arthur, a woman is dead. Murdered in her own home with seemingly impossible lock conditions. We need your expertise."

Authur fell silent, contemplating their words. His gaze shifted from Morgan to Derik, and then to the ground, as if grappling with an internal dilemma. Morgan studied Arthur's face, searching for any sign of deception. The lines around his eyes and the slump of his shoulders spoke of weariness, not malice. Internally, she weighed her instincts against the evidence—Arthur had no history of violence, and his surprise at the news of the murder seemed genuine. He wasn't behaving like a guilty man on the run. But perhaps his expertise could still prove invaluable to their investigation.

"Look," she began, her voice tinged with reluctant empathy. "I understand that you want to put your past behind you, but your knowledge could help us catch a killer. We don't need you to get involved in anything illegal—we just need information."

The breeze picked up, sending fallen leaves skittering down the street as Arthur considered Morgan's words. Finally, he sighed, his expression resigned.

"Alright," he said, meeting her gaze steadily. "I'll tell you what I can, but it won't be much. The best lockpicks can leave behind no trace—it's probably easier than people realize. You just need the right tools and enough practice."

"Is there anything specific we should look for?" Derik asked, his brow furrowed as he tried to parse Arthur's vague answer.

"Like I said, there might not be anything to find," Arthur replied, a hint of frustration creeping into his voice. "I'm sorry, but I can't help you. I just want to be left alone and continue my life away from the world of crime."

Morgan couldn't help feeling disappointed by Arthur's brief and ultimately unhelpful response, but she respected his desire to distance himself from his criminal past. She nodded, acknowledging his decision.

"Okay, Arthur. Thanks for your time."

As they watched him walk away, Morgan and Derik exchanged glances, both acutely aware of the weight of their unsolved case. But they couldn't force Arthur to help, and they'd have to find another lead to pursue—someone with the expertise they needed who was willing to cooperate. Morgan's determination flared like a dying ember brought back to life, her resolve only strengthened by this latest setback.

Arthur's retreating figure disappeared around a corner, leaving Morgan and Derik standing alone on the street, their breaths visible in the crisp autumn air. Morgan clenched her fists at her sides, her frustration bubbling to the surface. "Another dead end," she muttered, kicking a pebble that skittered across the pavement. "We're no closer to finding the killer than when we started."

Derik sighed, his gaze distant as he scanned the street. "Yeah, I know. But we can't let it get to us, Morgan. We'll find the connection we need—we just have to keep pushing forward."

"Right," Morgan agreed, her jaw set with determination. She glanced at her watch, noting the time. "Let's grab some lunch and regroup. Maybe we'll come up with something new."

CHAPTER TWELVE

A short walk brought Morgan and Derik to a quiet diner, its neon sign flickering with promises of comfort food, stirring Morgan's hunger. The bell above the door jingled cheerfully as they entered, announcing their presence to the handful of patrons scattered throughout the nearly empty establishment.

The worn red vinyl of the booth creaked as Morgan and Derik slid into their seats across from one another. A lone ceiling fan whirred above, doing little to dissipate the stifling midday heat that clung to their skin like a wet blanket. Morgan looked down at the laminated menu, but her mind was elsewhere. They ordered coffee and sandwiches, their voices barely audible over the hum of the refrigerator behind the counter.

As they waited for their food, the silence between them stretched on, punctuated only by the occasional clink of silverware against plates from the few other patrons in the diner. Morgan could feel the weight of the case pressing down on them, and she knew Derik felt it too. She glanced up to see him staring into his coffee cup, his green eyes clouded with worry. The lines around his eyes seemed more pronounced than ever, a testament to the toll this investigation had taken on both of them.

Unable to bear the silence any longer, Morgan looked out the window, watching as a stray piece of newspaper skittered down the street, carried along by a gentle breeze. Her thoughts kept circling back to their partnership and the strain it had been under lately. In spite of the betrayal that still hung between them like an unspoken secret, she found herself trusting Derik again—perhaps even more than before. But the nagging doubt remained, gnawing at the edge of her conscience: was she making a mistake by letting him back in?

"Rough day, huh?" Derik finally broke the silence, running a hand through his slick black hair. He mustered a weak smile, but it didn't quite reach his eyes. "Feels like we're hitting one dead end after another."

Morgan sighed, her gaze drifting back to him. "Yeah," she admitted, her voice barely above a whisper. "I just... I don't know,

Derik. I feel like we're so close to figuring this out, but every lead just slips through our fingers."

Morgan's hand tightened around her coffee cup, the warmth of the ceramic contrasting with the chill that had settled in her bones. Dark circles underlined Derik's green eyes, mirroring the exhaustion she felt creeping into every muscle. The case was a labyrinth they couldn't seem to navigate, and the walls were closing in.

"Damn it," Morgan muttered under her breath, slamming the coffee cup down on the table with more force than necessary. She caught Derik's gaze, her frustration and vulnerability laid bare. "We're running in circles, Derik. Every lead we chase ends up leading nowhere. We need something solid, something that can crack this case wide open."

Derik returned her stare with equal intensity, his forehead creased in concern. He nodded in agreement, his voice strained yet resolute. "I know, Morgan. It's getting to all of us. But we can't afford to give up. There has to be a connection, a piece of the puzzle we're missing."

Morgan's fingers absently traced the rim of her coffee cup, the dark liquid within reflecting the stormy emotions swirling inside her. The steam rose, fogging her vision for a moment, and she blinked, the world coming back into focus.

"It's not just the case, Derik," Morgan murmured, her eyes downcast. "Everything feels off. Us, our partnership. Thomas kidnapping Skunk. Nothing’s been right lately."

Derik leaned forward, the green of his eyes appearing almost luminous in the dim lighting of the diner. His tone was gentle but resolute as he spoke. "Morgan, we've been through a lot together. Maybe it's time we address the elephant in the room. The tension between us, it's not just about the case, is it?"

She met his gaze, her heart pounding in her chest as memories of their shared past flickered through her mind. The laughter, the camaraderie, and the foundation of trust that had once anchored them together now seemed precariously balanced atop a mountain of secrets and unspoken grievances.

Just as Morgan was about to answer, the waiter returned with their sandwiches, breaking the intensity of the moment. He set the plates down with a clatter, his cheerfulness jarring against the heaviness that hung in the air between them.

"Enjoy your meal," he said, oblivious to the turmoil beneath the surface.

"Thank you," Derik replied, his voice strained. As the waiter retreated, he took a deep breath, choosing his words carefully. "We used to be a great team, Morgan. I miss that. But we can't let our personal issues cloud our judgment. We owe it to the victims to solve this case, and we owe it to Skunk to find and save him."

Morgan stared at the sandwich before her, the lettuce wilting under the weight of the grilled bread. She picked at a stray tomato, her appetite lost amidst the storm of emotions brewing within her. Derik was right; they had an obligation to see this case through and to rescue Skunk from the clutches of Thomas Grady.

"Derik," she began, her voice quivering slightly as she pushed away her plate. "I know we need to put our personal issues aside, but it's hard. I want to trust you again, but I'm scared."

"I understand, Morgan," Derik replied softly, his fingertips brushing against hers in a fleeting moment of connection. "We'll work through it, together. We'll find the answers we need, and we'll bring Skunk home. I promise."

Morgan nodded, her eyes glistening with unshed tears. She looked out the window, watching as raindrops danced down the glass, leaving trails of sorrow in their wake. As much as she wanted to believe that they could repair the rift between them, part of her still feared that it might be impossible. But for now, they had a case to solve and a dog to save, and that had to be enough.

The silence between Morgan and Derik hung heavy in the air, a tangible barrier that threatened to suffocate them both. The diner's neon lights cast a dim glow over their untouched sandwiches, the vibrant colors failing to penetrate the darkness that enveloped them.

They began eating mechanically, each bite feeling like an obligation rather than nourishment. As they chewed, the clatter of dishes and the low hum of conversation from other patrons filled the void between them, serving as a stark reminder of how disconnected they had become from the world around them.

Morgan focused on the crumbs that fell onto the plate before her, the tiny fragments of bread forming an abstract pattern that she found oddly captivating. As she stared, her thoughts raced with doubts and fears, wondering if she could ever truly trust Derik again, or if their partnership was forever tainted by his past betrayal.

"Derik," she murmured, barely audible over the din of the diner. "I want to believe we can move past everything that's happened. But it's not going to be easy."

He looked at her, his expression a mixture of empathy and determination. "I know, Morgan. And I'm willing to fight for us, for our partnership. We've been through too much to let it all crumble now."

The soft hum of the diner's neon sign outside the window cast a gentle glow over their booth, casting shadows that seemed to dance in time with the low murmur of conversation. As Morgan stared down at her half-eaten sandwich, she found herself reflecting on the words they had just exchanged, feeling both relieved and apprehensive about the future of their partnership.

"Derik," she said, breaking the silence that had settled between them, "I want you to know that I'm willing to-" Her words were cut short by the sudden buzzing of her phone, the sound jarring against the muffled soundtrack of the diner.

Morgan's hand instinctively shot out to grab it from the table, her heart hammering in her chest as she recognized the number flashing across the screen. The Charlesberg precinct. She looked at Derik, his eyes mirroring her concern, before she pressed the phone to her ear and answered.

"Cross speaking," she said, her voice steady despite the unease creeping through her veins.

"Agent Cross, it's Officer Richards," the voice on the other end replied, sounding tense. "I'm afraid we've got some grim news. Another body has been found."

Morgan felt the blood drain from her face, leaving her cold and numb. She caught her breath, her knuckles whitening as she gripped the phone tightly. "Where?" she managed to choke out, her voice barely a whisper.

CHAPTER THIRTEEN

Morgan stepped out of the car, her eyes narrowing as she surveyed the upscale apartment building. Beside her, Derik unfolded his tall frame from the passenger seat, scanning the scene with an equally intense focus. Police officers had caution-taped off a section of the building, and residents stood outside, talking to law enforcement with worried expressions.

"Something feels off," Morgan muttered, more to herself than to Derik, as they approached the entrance. This was the first murder that had happened in an apartment building, not a house, suggesting a possible change of MO for the killer they were tracking. Not only that, but the killer's timeline had escalated, and Morgan couldn't shake the sense of dread that settled in her gut.

"Let's find out what we're dealing with," Derik said quietly, his professional demeanor masking the tiredness that seemed to haunt him these days.

Together, they hurried over to the officers on the scene, flashing their FBI badges as they approached. One of the officers, a young man with short-cropped hair, nodded at them before speaking. "Agent Cross, Agent Greene. We got a call from a neighbor who thought she heard a scream. When we arrived, we found Ms. Lucy Harrington, here on the first floor."

"Show us," Morgan commanded, her voice steady despite the uneasy feeling inside her. Her dark hair fell across her tattooed arms as she adjusted the cuffs of her shirt—a stark reminder of the years she spent in prison, framed for a murder she didn't commit.

The officer led them through the posh lobby and down a hallway lined with plush carpeting. As they reached the door to Lucy Harrington's apartment, Morgan paused, taking a deep breath to brace herself for the sight that awaited them. The memory of the last crime scene still haunted her—the lifeless body sprawled on the floor, blood pooling around the victim's head.

"Ready?" Derik asked, his gaze flicking over to Morgan. She nodded tersely, and together they stepped inside the apartment.

Morgan's heart pounded in her chest as she stepped further into the apartment. The air was heavy with tension, yet the space itself felt strangely homey. Soft lighting illuminated the open living room, and a plush rug invited barefoot steps. A part of Morgan wished she had more time to appreciate the tasteful decor, but her gut roiled as her eyes landed on the gruesome sight before her.

Lucy Harrington lay on the floor, her head bashed in, blood staining the rug beneath her. The contrast between the violence of the scene and the surrounding warmth only heightened Morgan's sense of unease.

"Damn," Derik muttered under his breath, echoing Morgan's thoughts.

"Let's focus on the doors," she said, her voice barely a whisper, as if speaking louder would somehow disturb the victim's spirit. Her dark eyes scanned the room, zeroing in on the entrance points.

"Good idea," Derik agreed. Together, they moved towards the front door that led into the hallway, Morgan's expert gaze scrutinizing the lock. It seemed undisturbed, but she knew better than to trust appearances alone.

"Check the porch door," she instructed, nodding towards the door that opened onto a small outdoor space. It was unusual for an apartment like this to have such a feature, and it only added to Morgan's suspicions.

As she examined the lock on the hallway door, her intuition whispered to her: these locks were their killer's canvas. Whoever had done this was an expert – someone who could slip in and out without leaving a trace.

"Hey, Morgan," Derik called from the porch door. "Take a look at this." His voice was tight with urgency, and she hurried over to join him.

The lock on the porch door was different – a key-based mechanism that seemed out of place. Morgan's pulse quickened as she realized this must be how the killer had entered and exited without being seen.

"Get a team on this," she said, her voice firm as she turned to Derik. "We need to preserve these locks, analyze them for any hidden clues."

"Right away," he replied, pulling out his phone to make the necessary calls.

As they waited for the forensic team to arrive, Morgan couldn't help but replay the scene over and over in her mind. Their killer was evolving, growing bolder with each attack – and it was up to her to stop them before more lives were lost. The weight of that responsibility settled heavily on her tattooed shoulders, but she knew there was no turning back now.

The silence in the apartment was oppressive; it seemed to swallow every breath, every whispered word as the forensic team moved through the crime scene. Morgan stood at the center of it all, her dark eyes sharp and focused as she directed their efforts.

"Remove these locks," she instructed, her voice low and steady. "Preserve them just like we did at Sarah's house." She couldn't shake the feeling that there was something vital hidden within those seemingly ordinary mechanisms – a secret that might lead them straight to the killer.

As the technicians set to work, Morgan began a slow circuit of the room. Every detail mattered, from the smallest fleck of dust to the very air they breathed. She had learned long ago to trust her instincts, and now those instincts were screaming at her to find what others might have missed.

It was then that she spotted it: a beer can, half-empty and abandoned on the coffee table. The sight sent a shiver down her spine, for it was an echo of previous crime scenes, a chilling reminder of the lives lost and the killer who remained at large.

"What do we have here?" she murmured, crouching down beside the table to examine the can more closely. The aluminum surface glinted in the dim light, innocent and damning all at once. Derik approached, his brow furrowing as he took in the scene.

"Another unattended drink," he said, his voice heavy with the weight of their shared history. "Just like before."

Morgan nodded, her mind racing as she catalogued every minuscule detail around the can. Her instincts screamed that this seemingly insignificant object held the key to solving the case, but she knew they would need more than gut feelings to bring down the monster responsible.

"Get this to the lab," she ordered, her voice clipped and precise. "Have them check for any substances that might be present. If we're lucky, it'll give us a lead."

Morgan watched the forensic team swabbing the beer can for residue, her jaw set with determination. The memory of Sarah's lifeless body flashed through her mind, and she couldn't help but imagine the unidentified substance coursing through her veins, a silent killer lurking beneath the surface. If this can held the key to identifying the substance, perhaps it would also reveal the connection between their victims—and bring them one step closer to the murderer.

"Make sure you compare the results with what we found in Sarah," she told the lead technician, her voice tight with urgency. "I want to know if there's any connection."

"Will do, Agent Cross," the technician replied, giving a quick nod before returning to his task.

With that taken care of, Morgan began her careful examination of the apartment, Derik shadowing her as they moved from room to room. She scrutinized every inch of the space, looking for signs of struggle or forced entry, her instincts guiding her like a compass needle seeking true north. In each room, she paid special attention to the security measures in place, comparing the complexity of locks and surveillance systems to those found at previous crime scenes.

"Seems our guy is getting bolder," she murmured to Derik, her eyes narrowing as she took note of the high-end security system installed within the apartment. "Or smarter."

"Or both," Derik agreed, his green eyes flicking around the room, taking in the various cameras that dotted the walls. "We'll have to go through the footage, see if anything stands out."

"Definitely," Morgan said, her mind already racing ahead to the potential evidence awaiting them on those digital recordings. "Let's finish up here and see what the cameras have to say."

***

Morgan stepped out of the crime scene, her boots squeaking against the polished marble floor of the upscale apartment building. The sharp scent of bleach hung heavy in the air, a stark contrast to the sinister acts that had taken place behind closed doors. To the left, residents huddled together in small groups, casting fearful glances at the yellow caution tape fluttering like restless ghosts.

Her eyes scanned the lobby, finally landing on a group of police officers gathered around an elderly man with silver hair and a kind, weathered face. She strode toward them, her FBI badge held up for all to see.

"Excuse me, I need to speak with the superintendent alone," Morgan announced, her tone firm and authoritative.

Reluctantly, the officers dispersed, leaving Morgan alone with the elderly man. She extended her hand, feeling the weight of her father's memory pressing down upon her. Would she ever be able to escape his shadow?

" Morgan Cross, FBI," she introduced herself, inwardly suppressing the pang of pain that came with every mention of her last name.

"Mark Fletcher," the man replied warmly, shaking her hand with a gentle grip. "I'm the superintendent of this building."

"Mr. Fletcher, does this building have security cameras on the outside?" Morgan asked, her voice steady despite the turmoil within her.

"Unfortunately, we don't have any exterior cameras," Mark replied, his expression apologetic. "But we do have them in the hallways."

Morgan nodded, her mind racing with possibilities. "Can you show me where I can access the footage?"

"Of course," Mark agreed, and together they set off down the hallway, their footsteps echoing in unison.

As they walked, Morgan felt a growing sense of unease. She had been so certain that the killer would be caught by now that she could put this case to rest and focus on rebuilding her own life. But with each new piece of evidence, it seemed as though the darkness only deepened.

Mark led Morgan into the security room, a small dimly lit space filled with monitors displaying grainy footage from various cameras throughout the apartment building. The hum of the equipment filled the air, creating an atmosphere of tense anticipation as Morgan took a seat in front of the central monitor.

"Thank you for your help, Mr. Fletcher," Morgan said, her fingers hovering over the keyboard as she prepared to review the footage. "I need to see any suspicious activity around Lucy Harrington's apartment yesterday."

"Of course, Agent Cross," Mark replied, pulling up a chair beside her. "Just let me know if you need assistance navigating the system."

Morgan nodded, her eyes fixed on the screen as she began to play back the footage. For a moment, all they saw were normal comings and goings—residents chatting, delivery people dropping off packages, the janitorial staff diligently performing their duties. But then her attention was caught by a particular scene.

"Wait, pause it there," Morgan instructed, her voice low and focused. Mark obliged, freezing the frame on a group of people led by a realtor through the hallway. Among them was Lucy, her face alive with curiosity as she followed the group.

"Who are these people?" Morgan asked, her eyes scanning the faces for any sign of recognition or malice.

"Ah, that's one of our realtors showing a special unit we have on the market," Mark explained, leaning in closer to get a better look. "Some residents like to tag along on those tours, especially if they're considering moving within the building. Lucy had only been living here for a couple of months, but she seemed eager to explore other options."

"Interesting," Morgan mused, tapping her fingers lightly on the desk as she considered this new information. It wasn't much, but it was another piece of the puzzle that could potentially lead her closer to the killer's identity. "Let's keep watching."

As they continued to review the footage, Morgan felt a growing sense of urgency. Time was running out, and with each passing moment, the killer moved further from her grasp. She needed a breakthrough, something that would lead her straight to the monster who had taken these women's lives.

"Keep your eyes sharp, Mr. Fletcher," she urged, her voice barely above a whisper. "We can't afford to miss anything."

Morgan studied the tour group carefully, her keen eyes taking in every detail of the individuals who accompanied Lucy. They were a diverse mix—elderly couples, middle-aged men and women, and even a few younger faces scattered throughout. The varying ages and appearances made it difficult to discern any obvious connections or potential suspects.

"Nothing promising here," she muttered under her breath, feeling her frustration mount. Her mind raced with the implications of the killer's changing MO. The more she thought about it, the more her gut told her that they were dealing with someone who was growing bolder—and more dangerous—by the day.

"Wait," Mark said suddenly, pausing the footage. "What do you make of this?"

The image on the screen now showed a man going door-to-door within the building, leaving fliers at each residence. Morgan leaned forward, her interest piqued.

"Who is he?" she asked, her voice tense with anticipation.

"Oliver," Mark replied. "He owns an antique store downtown and sometimes comes by to drop off fliers for his shop, trying to drum up business."

"An antique store owner, huh?" Morgan mused, her thoughts racing. An expert in antiques might have the knowledge and skills required to pick locks without leaving a trace. It wasn't much to go on, but it was a lead—one she couldn't afford to ignore.

Morgan eyed the man in the security footage, her instincts gnawing at her. "Does the building usually allow solicitation like this?" she asked Mark.

"Normally, no," he admitted, a hint of guilt coloring his voice. "But I made an exception for Oliver. His business has been struggling lately, and I felt bad for him. A lot of Charlesberg's older residents are moving out, and the younger crowd just isn't interested in antiques, especially not old ancient keys."

"Keys?" Morgan seized on the word, her heart rate picking up. Her mind raced with the possibility that they were chasing a killer who was an expert on locks, perhaps even someone with intimate knowledge of antique locking mechanisms. She could almost feel the phantom weight of the handcuffs that had once bound her wrists, the memory of her own imprisonment fueling her determination to catch this murderer.

"Can I see one of these fliers?" she asked, her voice taut with urgency.

"Of course," Mark replied, pulling open a cabinet drawer and rifling through its contents. He extracted a folded piece of paper and handed it to Morgan, who unfolded it with trembling hands.

The flier advertised Oliver's shop, complete with an assortment of images showcasing various antique items. And there, among the display of relics, was an array of intricately designed, ancient keys. Morgan's pulse quickened as she scanned the flier, noting the emphasis on the keys, each one a potential tool in the hands of a skilled lock-picker.

"Thank you," she said, her voice barely more than a whisper as she clutched the flier tightly in her ink-stained fingers. To anyone else, this flier may have seemed like an innocent advertisement for a struggling business. But to Morgan, it was a potential lifeline—a lead that could bring her one step closer to catching the elusive killer who had been terrorizing Charlesberg.

CHAPTER FOURTEEN

The sun dipped toward the horizon, casting a dim orange glow over the quiet streets of Charlesberg. Morgan's heart pounded in her chest as she and Derik stood outside a peculiar antique store. The peeling paint on its windowed front revealed years of neglect, a visual representation of the dying market for ancient relics in the town.

Morgan couldn't shake the feeling that they were on the right track this time, that the answer to their case lay hidden behind these dusty windows. And if her instincts were correct, then each moment they wasted was another step closer to the killer's next strike.

As they pushed open the creaky door, the chime of an old-fashioned bell announced their arrival. Stepping into the cluttered shop felt like entering another world—a place where time had come to a standstill. Dust motes danced in the air, illuminated by the fading sunlight filtering through the grimy windows. The smell of musty wood and age-old secrets filled their nostrils, masking any trace of the modern world beyond the shop's walls.

The dimly lit store seemed to close in around them as they ventured further, the weight of dusty history pressing down on their shoulders. Morgan's gaze drifted across the labyrinthine aisles, each one lined with artifacts that whispered secrets of bygone eras. The faint scent of old wood and the distant tick-tock of an aged clock filled the silence, heightening her senses.

At last, they found him. Hunched over a workbench at the back of the store, Oliver meticulously polished an ancient key, its ornate design shimmering beneath his steady hand. His brow furrowed in concentration, he appeared oblivious to the agents' solemn purpose.

"Oliver?" Derik called out, breaking the stillness.

"Ah," he looked up, startled. "Yes, that's me."

Morgan's stomach churned as she watched the man handle the key, the metal glinting ominously in the dim light. Could he be the one? The thought gnawed at her insides, fuelling the fire of determination that burned within her.

"Allow me to introduce ourselves," Morgan said, flashing her badge. "I'm Special Agent Morgan Cross, and this is my partner, Derik Greene. We're here to ask you some questions."

"Of course, of course," Oliver replied hastily, setting the key aside and wiping his hands on a rag. His eyes darted between the agents, betraying a hint of unease. "What can I help you with?"

"Actually, we'd like to know more about your activities today," Derik interjected, his calm demeanor a stark contrast to Morgan's bristling intensity.

"Today?" Oliver's fingers twitched nervously, betraying the urgency in his voice. "Well, I've been here all day, working on my keys. Not much business, as you can see." He gestured to the empty store, his expression a mix of defensiveness and annoyance.

Morgan studied him carefully, her instincts whispering a warning that something wasn't quite right about this man. She clenched her jaw, her mind racing with questions that demanded answers. And she would not stop until she found them.

"Tell us, Mr. Oliver," Morgan said, her voice steady and cold. "Do you know anything about a series of break-ins happening in Charlesberg?"

"Break-ins?" He seemed genuinely surprised. "No, I can't say I do. I'm just a simple antique dealer."

"Is that so?" Morgan replied, her eyes narrowing as she caught the flicker of fear in his gaze. "Earlier today, you were at an apartment building handing out fliers, correct?" Morgan asked, her voice sharp and probing.

"Y-yes, that's right," Oliver stammered, his fingers drumming an anxious rhythm on the counter. "I was promoting my shop, trying to drum up some business. It's been slow lately."

"Understandable," Morgan replied icily. "Now, we'd like to know more about your visit there, especially considering recent events."

"Recent events?" He frowned, confusion clouding his features.

"Perhaps you already know this, but one of the residents you delivered a flier to is dead," Morgan informed him, her eyes boring into his as she observed his reaction.

"Dead?" Oliver repeated, a flicker of fear crossing his face before he managed to compose himself. "That's... I had no idea. Terrible news, really. But what does it have to do with me?"

"Someone has been breaking into women's homes in Charlesberg without leaving any trace of their presence," Morgan explained, watching him closely. "It's almost as if they're... an expert on locks and keys." She tilted her head slightly, nodding toward the key he had been working on earlier.

The weight of her words hung heavy in the air, and Oliver's hand trembled as he instinctively reached for the old key. It slipped from his grasp, clattering onto the floor with a jarring echo.

"Look, I just handed out fliers," he insisted, a sheen of sweat forming on his brow. "I don't know anything about those break-ins or that woman's death. I'm just an antique dealer trying to make ends meet."

Morgan studied him for a moment, her instincts screaming that there was more to this man than met the eye. She could feel it in her bones - the desperate urgency in his voice, the evasiveness of his words - something wasn't right. But what was he hiding? And could it be the key to solving this case?

"Are you suggesting I had something to do with those crimes?" Oliver's voice grew defensive, his eyes darting from Morgan to Derik and back again. "I've never hurt anyone in my life! I'm just an antique salesman, trying to keep my store afloat."

Morgan observed the beads of sweat forming on his forehead, the way his hands trembled ever so slightly. She had learned to trust her gut over the years, and it was telling her that Oliver knew more than he was letting on.

"Is that all you are, Oliver?" Morgan asked, her voice like ice. "Just an innocent salesman?"

As she spoke, she could see the panic rise in Oliver's eyes, his breathing becoming more labored. In a moment of sheer desperation, he suddenly bolted toward the back of the shop, disappearing through a hidden doorway. The abruptness of his flight sent a jolt through both agents.

"Derik, come on!" Morgan shouted as she sprinted after Oliver. What was he hiding? Had they finally found the man responsible for these brutal crimes?

The chase led them through the cluttered labyrinth of the antique store, narrow aisles filled with delicate trinkets and forgotten treasures. Every step felt like navigating a minefield, each piece a potential obstacle that threatened to trip them up or shatter beneath their feet.

Morgan's heart pounded in her chest, adrenaline coursing through her veins as she tried to close the distance between herself and Oliver.

She couldn't afford to let him escape; too many lives were at stake, and she refused to let another woman suffer at the hands of this monster.

"Stop, Oliver!" Morgan yelled, her voice echoing off the walls of the cramped space. "You can't run forever!"

But even as she shouted, a part of her wondered: Was she right to pursue him so relentlessly? Could Oliver truly be the key to stopping these brutal killings, or was her determination blinding her judgment?

"Derik," she panted, "do you have eyes on him?"

"Negative," Derik replied, his own breath heavy with exertion. "But he can't have gone far. Keep going, Morgan. We'll catch him."

With renewed resolve, Morgan pressed on, her eyes scanning the shadowy corners of the shop as she chased after the enigmatic figure who held the answers she so desperately sought. The hunt was on, and she would not rest until the truth was finally revealed.

The sharp tang of sweat and fear filled the air, intensifying as Morgan and Derik cornered Oliver in a narrow aisle lined with antique keys. The only exit was blocked by their determined forms, leaving him no choice but to confront them head-on.

"Stay back!" Oliver snarled, his eyes wild with desperation as he grabbed a handful of keys from a nearby shelf, brandishing them like makeshift weapons. "You don't know what you're dealing with!"

"Put those down, Oliver," Morgan said firmly, her voice a calm contrast to the chaos that surrounded them. "We just want to talk."

"Like hell you do!" With a defiant cry, Oliver lunged at them, keys swinging through the air in a frantic arc. Morgan and Derik moved in unison, ducking beneath the improvised projectiles, before surging forward to subdue their suspect.

"Derik, now!" Morgan called out, and together they tackled Oliver, their combined strength forcing him to the ground amidst a cacophony of clattering keys. The metallic symphony rang out as they grappled, each key a testament to the countless lives touched by their intricate mechanisms.

"Get off me!" Oliver yelled, his body thrashing beneath their grip. But even as he fought, Morgan could see the fear in his eyes, the raw terror that drove him to such desperate measures.

"Give it up, Oliver," she growled, locking her arm around his neck. "You're not getting away this time."

"Please... I didn't do anything..." His voice was choked, barely audible above the din of their struggle. "You've got it all wrong..."

"Then why run?" Derik asked, his tone laced with suspicion as he pinned Oliver's flailing limbs. "Why put up such a fight if you're innocent?"

"Because... because I'm scared, alright?" Oliver's voice cracked, his gaze darting between the cold faces of his captors. "You come in here, accusing me of... of those horrible things! I didn't know what else to do."

As they held him down, Morgan searched for the truth in those panicked eyes. Was he really just a frightened man caught in the crossfire of their relentless pursuit? Or was there something more sinister lurking beneath that veneer of fear?

"Oliver," she said softly, her grip on him never wavering, "if you have nothing to hide, then let us help you clear your name. But if you're guilty, you can't escape justice forever."

In that moment, the fight seemed to drain from Oliver, his body going limp as he stared up at her with a mixture of resignation and defeat. Morgan could only hope that she had made the right decision—that in pursuing Oliver so tenaciously, she hadn't allowed her desire for justice to blind her to the truth.

Morgan and Derik managed to subdue Oliver, the room now eerily silent except for their labored breathing. As she held him down, her mind raced with new theories and possibilities, daring to hope that they had finally caught the killer this time. They exchanged a glance, silently acknowledging the weight of what was at stake.

"Let's get him to the station," Morgan said tersely, her grip firm on Oliver's arm.

"Right behind you," Derik replied.

CHAPTER FIFTEEN

The cold, sterile walls of the Charlesberg police station closed around them like an unforgiving vice as Morgan and Derik escorted Oliver into the interrogation room. The atmosphere was oppressive, the tension palpable. Their colleagues scrutinized their every move through the one-way mirror, their gaze as sharp as broken glass.

Morgan ignored the watchful eyes, focused solely on the task at hand: extracting the truth from Oliver. She took her seat across from him, the chill of the metal chair seeping through her clothes to her skin. Derik mirrored her position, his tall frame casting a long shadow on the concrete floor.

"Alright, Oliver," Morgan began, her voice steady but ice-cold. "You're going to tell us everything you know about the murders, and we're going to figure out if you're guilty or not."

"Like I told you before, I didn't do it!" Oliver insisted, running a shaky hand through his disheveled hair. "I'm just an antique salesman! I don't know anything about any murders!"

"Then explain your actions earlier today," Derik interjected, his voice cool and measured. "Why run? Why fight us?"

"Because I was scared!" Oliver snapped back, his eyes darting between the two agents. "You came accusing me of horrible things, I didn't know what else to do."

Morgan studied his face intently, searching for any hint of deception. Her mind buzzed with questions – was he truly just a frightened man caught in the crossfire? Or was there something more sinister lurking beneath that veneer of fear?

"Oliver," she said softly, her gaze never leaving his face, "if you have nothing to hide, then let us help you clear your name. But if you're guilty, you can't escape justice forever."

Morgan leaned forward, her dark eyes fixed on Oliver's face as she slid a glossy photograph across the table. It showed a crumpled locksmith flyer bearing his company logo, found inside Lucy Harrington's apartment. Oliver's gaze flicked to the image and back to Morgan, defiance brewing in his narrowed eyes.

"Explain this," Morgan demanded. "You left one of your flyers at Lucy Harrington's place, but that's not all." She pulled out another photograph, this time from Sarah's house, revealing an identical flyer lying on the kitchen counter. "We found another one at Sarah's house."

Oliver clenched his jaw, his hands gripping the edge of the table as he shook his head. "I hand out flyers all over town. That doesn't make me a killer."

"Maybe not," Morgan acknowledged, her voice low and dangerous. "But it does make you someone who knows a lot about locks and antique keys. Someone who could easily pick a lock without leaving a trace."

"Are you serious?" He scoffed, his face growing red with indignation. "This is ridiculous! I'm just trying to keep my business alive, and now you're accusing me of murder?"

Morgan noted his body language, the way he avoided direct eye contact and unconsciously tapped his foot on the floor. She had spent years observing people, learning to read the subtle signs of deception and guilt. And although Oliver vehemently denied any involvement, there was something about his behavior that made her question his innocence.

"Two women are dead, Oliver," Morgan reminded him, her voice softening ever so slightly. "If you have nothing to hide, help us find the person responsible."

"I barely knew them," Oliver insisted, his hands gripping the edge of the table as if it were a lifeline. "I only gave them my fliers, just like everyone else in town."

"Everyone else in town?" Morgan repeated, narrowing her eyes. She could see the sweat beading on his forehead, betraying his fear. "That's an interesting choice of words. It doesn't make you a murderer, but it does raise some questions."

"Look, I'm just trying to keep my business afloat," he replied, his voice cracking ever so slightly. "I'm passionate about antiques, and I've spent years collecting and restoring these beautiful pieces. But people don't appreciate them anymore. So yeah, I send out fliers to everyone, hoping they'll take an interest. That doesn't make me a killer!"

Morgan observed him closely, her intuition whispering that there was more to this man than met the eye. But she needed proof, something concrete to connect him to the murders. "And you never interacted with either woman outside of giving them your fliers?"

"Never," Oliver replied, though his gaze wavered for a moment, sending a chill down Morgan's spine.

Derik stepped in, his calm demeanor a stark contrast to Morgan's relentless questioning. "Let's talk about your schedule, Oliver," he said, his green eyes meeting the suspect's gaze. "Can you walk us through what you did on the days the victims were killed?"

"Like I said, I was handing out fliers," Oliver muttered, his answers growing vaguer with each passing moment. "I don't remember the exact times or anything. I was just trying to drum up some business."

"Oliver, we're trying to help you here," Derik continued, his voice gentle but firm. "But we need you to be honest with us. Anything you can tell us, even the smallest detail, could make a difference."

Oliver's eyes darted around the room, and for a moment, Morgan thought she saw a flicker of defeat in his gaze. But just as quickly, he seemed to steel himself, his defiance returning with full force. "I've told you everything I know," he insisted stubbornly. "I didn't kill those women."

Morgan's jaw tightened as she reached into a manila folder, extracting the glossy photographs of the victims. She imagined their families, their futures stolen from them, and her resolve hardened. With a calculated motion, she slid the pictures across the table towards Oliver.

"Take a good look at these faces, Oliver," she said, her voice icy. "These women didn't deserve to die."

Oliver hesitated before picking up the photos, his hands trembling ever so slightly. As he studied each image, Morgan watched his brow furrow and his defiance crumble, replaced by something akin to fear. Yet, through it all, he continued to maintain his innocence.

"I—I didn't do this," he stammered, his eyes glistening with unshed tears. "I swear."

Morgan leaned in, her dark tattoos shifting beneath her sleeves as she placed her hands on the table. "If you're not the killer, then why are you so scared, Oliver? What are you hiding?"

Oliver's gaze darted between the photos and Morgan's unwavering stare, sweat beading along his forehead. Finally, with a shaky exhale, he cracked.

"Alright, fine!" he blurted out. "Some of the antiques I have... they aren't exactly legal. I've stolen them. That's why I ran when you questioned me. But I'm not a killer!"

Morgan felt a flare of triumph mixed with frustration. This confession gave them leverage but did little to confirm or deny his involvement in the murders. She exchanged a glance with Derik, whose calm demeanor seemed to mirror her own tumultuous thoughts.

"Stolen antiques, Oliver?" Derik asked, his voice measured. "That's quite a risk to take just for some extra business."

Oliver wiped his sweaty palms on his pants, his gaze shifting between Morgan and Derik. "Look, I'm not proud of it, but I've never hurt anyone. I'm just trying to keep my store afloat."

Morgan's eyes narrowed, her mind racing with the implications of Oliver's confession. It was possible that his desperation had led him to theft, but not murder... yet something gnawed at her gut, urging her not to let go just yet. She exchanged a troubled look with Derik, whose own expression mirrored her unease.

"Oliver, we're going to need more than your word on this," she warned, fingering the edge of a crime scene photo. "And if we find any connection between you and these murders—"

A sudden knock on the door interrupted her mid-sentence. Morgan's head snapped around, annoyance flashing in her dark eyes. The door cracked open, revealing a young officer looking equal parts apologetic and anxious. "Agent Cross? I have news that can't wait."

"Alright," she replied tersely, pulling herself away from the table and striding out into the hallway with Derik hot on her heels. "What is it?"

"Ma'am," the officer began, his voice shaking slightly under her intense gaze. "We've reviewed security footage from the area surrounding Lucy Harrington's apartment. We found footage of Oliver handing out fliers at another residence during the exact time the neighbor called about the scream they heard in Lucy's apartment."

Morgan felt her heart sink as the implications settled in. She glanced back through the window at Oliver, who sat slumped in the interrogation room, his face pale and drawn. If he wasn't their killer, then they were no closer to finding the monster responsible for those deaths. And with each passing moment, the threat loomed larger, casting its shadow over Charlesberg.

"Damn it," she muttered, rubbing her temples as frustration welled up within her. The crushing weight of responsibility weighed heavily on her shoulders—the lives of innocent women hung in the balance, and she was no closer to saving them.

"Agent Cross," Derik murmured, his green eyes filled with understanding and concern. "We'll find him. We just have to keep looking."

"Right," she agreed, steeling herself for the task ahead. She turned back to the officer, her voice firm. "Thank you for the information. Keep searching for any other possible connections to the crime scenes, and let me know immediately if anything turns up."

As the officer nodded and hurried away, Morgan and Derik shared a weary look. This dead-end hurt. It stung like hell, but they couldn't afford to dwell on it. Time was running short, and they needed to find the killer before he struck again.

"Let's regroup," she said, determination burning in her veins. "We've dealt with setbacks before, Derik. We'll find this bastard, even if we have to tear Charlesberg apart brick by brick."

CHAPTER SIXTEEN

Morgan gripped the steering wheel, knuckles white and jaw clenched as she navigated the streets of Charlesberg. Beside her, Derik stared out the window, his green eyes distant, while the silence between them grew heavy. The investigation was slipping through their fingers, each lead proving to be just another dead end.

She glanced at him, noting the determination in his gaze. It was a look she had come to rely on, even after his past betrayal. It was true that she was starting to forgive him, but trust was not easily rebuilt.

"We need to dig deeper into the lives of the victims," Morgan said. "Lucy Harrington is our most recent case. Let's see what we can find out about her. Her mom lives in the next town over. It's not far. We should head there."

As they drove toward the neighboring town, Morgan couldn't help but feel the weight of their responsibility pressing down on her. She was no stranger to hardship, having been framed for murder and spending ten years in prison. But this case, this killer, seemed to elude them at every turn. And with each passing day, the stakes only grew higher.

"Derik," Morgan began, her voice barely above a whisper, "do you ever wonder if we're really cut out for this? What if we can't stop this monster?"

"Hey," Derik responded, gripping her shoulder a bit tighter. "We've faced worse, and we're still here. We're going to find this bastard, and we're going to make sure he never hurts anyone again."

Morgan's dark eyes met his, the faintest hint of a smile tugging at the corners of her tattooed lips. "You're right," she said, steeling herself for what lay ahead. "Let's go talk to Lucy's mom."

***

The afternoon sun cast a warm glow on the quiet suburban street where Lucy's mother, Linda, lived. As Morgan parked the car outside the modest, single-story home, she felt a pang of guilt for intruding on such a peaceful scene with the heavy weight of their investigation.

They exited the car and approached the house, taking in the well-tended flower beds that lined the walkway. Despite the modesty of the neighborhood compared to the ostentatious wealth of Charlesberg, it was clear that love and care had been put into creating a welcoming home. Morgan found herself wondering what had driven Lucy away from this place and into the heart of danger.

As they reached the front door, Derik raised his hand to knock. Before his knuckles could make contact, the door swung open to reveal a middle-aged woman who looked as though she'd just emerged from a storm—her eyes red-rimmed and puffy, her hair disheveled. The broken expression on her face made it all too evident that she had already received the news of her daughter's passing.

"Mrs. Harrington?" Derik asked gently, concern washing over his tired features. "I'm Agent Derik Greene, and this is my partner, Agent Morgan Cross. We're with the FBI."

Linda stared blankly at them for a moment before her gaze shifted to Morgan. In that instant, something seemed to click, and she choked back a sob before nodding and stepping aside to let them in.

"Please," she whispered, her voice trembling. "Come in."

As they crossed the threshold, Morgan couldn't shake the feeling that they were intruding during one of the darkest moments of this woman's life. But she also knew that they couldn't afford to waste any time—their best chance at catching the killer lay in uncovering every piece of information they could about his victims.

"Mrs. Harrington, we're so sorry for your loss," Morgan said quietly as they settled into the cozy living room. "We're doing everything we can to find the person responsible."

Linda nodded, wiping her eyes with a tissue. "I know you are, Agent Cross. And I want to help however I can." Her voice was shaky, but there was a determination behind her words that spoke of a mother's love and the need for justice.

Morgan met her gaze, her own resolve strengthened by Linda's courage. Together, they would find the answers they sought, no matter how painful the journey may be.

Linda's hands trembled as she clutched a framed photograph of Lucy, her eyes shining with unshed tears. She was trying to hold herself together, but the cracks were visible in her fragile smile.

"Can I get you anything?" she asked, glancing from Morgan to Derik. "Coffee, maybe?"

"Thank you, Mrs. Harrington," Morgan replied gently. "But we're fine for now."

Linda nodded and placed the photo back on the mantel, her gaze lingering on the innocent face of her daughter. The walls were adorned with pictures of Lucy growing up—laughing as she played in the park, dancing at her high school prom, beaming proudly at her college graduation. Each memory seemed to mock the brutal reality of her death, fueling the fire inside Morgan.

"Mrs. Harrington," Derik began, his voice soft and solemn. "We understand this is an extraordinarily difficult time for you. But any information you can provide about Lucy might help us find the person responsible."

"Of course," Linda said, forcing a deep breath. "I'll do whatever I can to help." Her voice cracked, but she straightened her spine and locked eyes with Morgan, the light of determination flickering within them.

"Lucy was such a bright, driven young woman," she continued, her voice steadier now. "She moved here to chase her dreams. And now…" Linda trailed off, the pain too great to voice aloud.

Seated in the cozy living room, surrounded by family photos and framed dance recitals, Morgan couldn't help but feel the stark contrast between this warm sanctuary and the cold reality of Lucy's fate. Linda sat opposite them, clutching a tissue in her trembling hands, her eyes red-rimmed from unshed tears.

"Lucy always dreamt of becoming a famous dancer," Linda shared in a voice laced with pride. "She had this fire inside her that just wouldn't quit. When she heard about the dance studio in Charlesberg, she knew she had to be there. It was even better than some of the studios we have back in Dallas."

Derik nodded, his expression sympathetic. "It sounds like she was very talented and determined."

Linda smiled softly, caught in a memory. "She was. No matter how many times she fell, she always got back up. She believed she could make it, and I believed in her too." Her voice broke at the end, and Derik reached over to offer a comforting touch on her arm.

Morgan leaned forward, her mind working through the information they had gathered so far. "Mrs. Harrington, before Lucy moved to Charlesberg, did she ever mention experiencing any break-ins or feeling like she was being stalked?"

Linda shook her head, her brow furrowing in confusion. "No, not that I'm aware of. Why do you ask?"

"Part of our investigation involves looking into any potential threats or suspicious activities that might have occurred before the victims' deaths," Morgan explained, attempting to maintain a delicate balance between transparency and preserving Linda's fragile emotional state.

"Of course," Linda said, her voice barely more than a whisper. "I wish I could give you more. I'd do anything in my power to help catch the monster who did this to my baby girl."

The sudden vibration of Morgan's phone disrupted the somber atmosphere in the living room. She glanced at the screen, noting the call was from the police precinct. "Excuse me for a moment," she said softly to Linda, standing up and stepping away.

"Cross speaking," she answered, her voice taking on a professional tone despite the torrent of emotions swirling within her.

"Agent Cross, this is Officer Ramirez," came the frantic voice on the other end. "I've just received a letter at the precinct, and we… we think it's from the killer."

Morgan's heart jumped into her throat, her grip tightening around the phone. "We'll be right there." She ended the call and turned towards Derik and Linda. "Mrs. Harrington, I'm so sorry, but we have to go. We'll be in touch if we need any further information."

"Of course," Linda said with a weak nod, wiping away fresh tears. "Please, find whoever did this."

"We will," Morgan promised, her eyes locking with Derik's as they hurried out of the house.

CHAPTER SEVENTEEN

The bright fluorescent lights of the forensics lab at FBI headquarters cast an eerie glow over the scene as Morgan and Derik entered, their faces taut with determination. Forensic analysts were hunched over a table, poring over a single sheet of paper that lay under the sterile beam of a desk lamp.

"Agent Cross, Agent Greene," one of the analysts greeted, gesturing towards the mysterious letter. "This is what came in. It's been handled with gloves, so we're still trying to get some prints, but so far, nothing."

Morgan felt a shiver run down her spine as she examined the letter, her mind racing to decipher its meaning. The scrawled handwriting seemed to taunt her with its hidden intent. She glanced at Derik, who was studying it just as intently.

"Any idea what it says?" Derik asked, his voice low and controlled.

"Not yet," the analyst replied. "It's like a code or something. We're working on it."

Morgan stared at the cryptic message, her heart pounding in her chest. Whoever had written this held the key to understanding the killer's motives, but it remained frustratingly out of reach. She closed her eyes for a moment, trying to focus her thoughts, then opened them again, her gaze fixated on the letter.

"Keep us updated on any progress," she told the analysts, her voice firm. "We need to crack this before another life is lost."

As she turned away from the table, her mind churned with possibilities, each more horrifying than the last. The weight of the case bore down on her, threatening to crush her spirit, but she refused to let it break her. She would see this through, no matter the cost. And with each step closer to the truth, she hoped to restore justice for the victims and their families.

Morgan's eyes narrowed as she studied the letter under the microscope, the ink on the aged parchment seeming to mock her with its elusive meaning. An expert stood beside her, manipulating the infrared scanner that hovered over the paper, casting a ghostly light upon the coded message.

"Anything yet?" Derik asked from where he stood across the room, his voice tense with anticipation. He was busy coordinating efforts with field officers through his earpiece, making sure all possible resources were being utilized in their investigation.

"Nothing solid," Morgan replied, frustration creeping into her voice. "We've tried several decryption methods, but each one leads to a dead end." She looked up at the analyst, who shook his head in agreement. The tension in the air was palpable - it felt like they were racing against time, and every failed attempt only served to heighten the urgency of the situation.

"Keep trying," Derik urged, his green eyes flicking between Morgan and the letter. "There has to be something we're missing."

Morgan clenched her jaw, nodding silently as she refocused on the cryptic text. Her mind raced, connecting dots and analyzing patterns, desperately trying to pry open the secrets hidden within the taunting lines.

"Have you considered that it might be an anagram?" the analyst suggested, adjusting the scanner settings.

"Already tried," Morgan shot back, her voice terse. The weight of the case threatened to suffocate her, pressing down on her chest like a vise. The clock was ticking, and they were no closer to stopping the killer than when they had first started.

"Alright, let's take a step back," the analyst said, sensing Morgan's mounting frustration. "Maybe if we approach it from a different angle..."

"Fine," Morgan sighed, rubbing her temples as she forced herself to take a deep breath. "Just let me know if anything changes."

"Will do," the analyst replied, his gaze returning to the letter.

Morgan crossed the room and joined Derik, who was still liaising with field officers. She could see the weariness in his eyes as he updated them on the cryptic message situation. Morgan knew that both their pasts were catching up to them - her time in prison and his struggles with alcoholism - but they were in this together, and they would see it through to the end.

"Anything new?" she asked, leaning against the wall beside him.

"Nothing yet," Derik admitted, his voice low. "But we're not giving up."

"Neither am I," Morgan replied, determination flaring within her. She glanced back at the letter, the coded message taunting her like a specter. They would uncover its secrets - and bring the killer to justice.

Hours stretched into an endless loop of frustration and defeat as Morgan, Derik, and the forensics team attempted to crack the code hidden within the letter. With every failed attempt at decryption, the atmosphere in the forensics lab grew heavier, suffocating them beneath an unrelenting sense of dread. Time was slipping through their fingers like sand, and Morgan couldn't shake the feeling that they were playing a losing game.

"Let's try running it through the frequency analysis software again," one of the analysts suggested, fatigue seeping into her voice. "Maybe we missed something the first time around."

"Fine," Morgan snapped, her patience fraying at the edges. "But we've tried that twice already. I don't see how—"

"Sometimes it takes a few passes," the analyst interrupted, a hint of steel in her tone. She wasn't going to back down, despite the mounting pressure. "We can't afford to miss anything, Agent Cross. We owe it to the victims."

Morgan clenched her fists, her knuckles turning white. The analyst was right, but that didn't make the truth any easier to swallow. As the minutes ticked by, the weight of their failure bore down on her, threatening to crush her spirit.

"Derik," she called out, unable to bear the oppressive silence any longer. "I need a break. I'm stepping outside for a moment."

"Take your time," he replied, his gaze never leaving the screen in front of him. "I'll keep everyone updated."

Morgan slipped out of the lab, the door sealing shut behind her with a soft hiss. The sterile fluorescent lighting of the hallway did little to lift her spirits as she leaned against the cool wall, allowing its icy touch to seep into her overheated skin.

"Damn it," she muttered under her breath, raking a hand through her dark hair. "We're going in circles."

In the solitude of the empty corridor, she allowed herself a moment of vulnerability, closing her eyes and taking slow, measured breaths in an attempt to calm her racing thoughts. The memories of the victims haunted her -- their faces etched into her mind's eye, a chilling reminder of what was at stake.

"Every clue leads us further into this damned maze," she whispered, her voice barely audible even to her own ears. "How are we supposed to find our way out?"

Morgan knew that the answer lay hidden within the cryptic message, taunting her from just beyond her reach. And as long as it remained concealed, the killer would continue his twisted game, leaving a trail of broken lives in his wake.

Determined to break the impasse, she pushed away from the wall and strode back toward the lab, her resolve steeled once more. They had to keep trying for the sake of those who had already been lost — and for the countless others who might still be saved.

The door swung open with a soft creak, and Derik stepped into the dimly lit corridor. His green eyes found Morgan's troubled gaze, concern etching lines into his usually smooth features. He leaned against the wall beside her, a quiet solidarity in their shared frustration.

"Maybe it's time we brought in an expert," he suggested gently, his voice low and intimate in the enclosed space. "Someone who can help us crack this code."

Morgan hesitated, chewing on her lower lip as she weighed his proposal. Trust didn't come easily to her, especially when it came to this case – but she couldn't deny that they were running out of options. With a reluctant sigh, she nodded her agreement.

"Alright," she acquiesced, her voice heavy with the weight of their circumstances. "Who do you have in mind?"

"One of the Charlesberg police officers mentioned a guy who's helped them with similar cases in the past," Derik explained, his fingers tapping a rhythmic pattern against the cold wall. "He's a retired profiler living nearby. I can't vouch for him personally, but at this point, we need all the help we can get."

"Desperate times," Morgan muttered, echoing his earlier sentiment. She knew that their window of opportunity was shrinking by the hour, and if an outside perspective could break them free from this labyrinthine nightmare, she had to be willing to take that risk.

"Exactly." Derik straightened up, the determination in his eyes resonating with her own. "I'll make some calls, see if we can set up a meeting."

"Good," Morgan replied, pushing off from the wall and facing her partner. "Let's hope he can give us the edge we need to catch this monster."

As they made their way back towards the lab, Morgan felt a flicker of hope begin to burn within her. Bringing in an expert was a gamble, but it was one she was willing to take if it meant saving lives.

"Derik," she said softly, her voice barely audible above the hum of fluorescent lights overhead. "Thank you. I know I can be... stubborn at times."

He glanced over at her, a ghost of a smile playing at the corners of his mouth. "You're welcome, Morgan. We're in this together, remember?"

In that moment, their eyes locked, and something unspoken passed between them – a shared understanding that, despite everything, they were united in their quest for justice. And with that knowledge firmly in hand, they continued on, ready to face whatever challenges lay ahead.

CHAPTER EIGHTEEN

The air was thick with the smell of rust and mildew as the man meticulously arranged his lockpicking tools on a solid wooden table. The dimly lit room seemed to shiver in anticipation, each flicker of the single light bulb casting sinister shadows on the walls. The rhythmic clinking of metal against wood punctured the silence, echoing through the confined space like the tolling of distant church bells.

In this isolated and grim lair, a haven for a twisted mind, blueprints of the victims' homes lay scattered haphazardly, each marked with detailed annotations that spoke of countless hours of meticulous study. But it was the memento that held the man's attention now – Lucy's dance pendant, a small, gleaming trinket that had once been a symbol of her dreams.

"Such a shame," he murmured, running a calloused finger over the pendant's smooth surface. "So much potential, wasted."

As he carefully polished the pendant with a soft cloth, his eyes betrayed both pride and obsession. There was an unnerving tenderness in the way he held the fragile keepsake, cradling it as if it were a precious gemstone rather than a grim trophy from a life brutally cut short.

"Lucy...you would've danced so beautifully," he whispered, almost to himself. "But you couldn't unlock your own potential."

He set the pendant aside, turning his attention back to his task. Each lockpicking tool had its specific purpose, and he knew them all intimately – just as he knew the secrets hidden within each lock he encountered. With a satisfied nod, he surveyed his equipment one last time before shifting his gaze to a blueprint spread out before him.

There, among the myriad of sketches and notes, a new challenge beckoned. A fresh canvas upon which he could display his mastery of locks. And as he traced the lines of the blueprint with his finger, his mind began to race, planning out his next "test" in vivid detail.

"But first," he thought, "I must ensure that every detail is perfect. That nothing is left to chance."

And so, as the shadows lengthened and the room grew colder, the man continued his macabre preparations. Unseen, unheard, and utterly determined to prove himself once more as the ultimate locksmith.

The dim light danced eerily across the polished surface of Lucy's dance pendant as he held it up, admiring his handiwork. The man's eyes sparkled with a twisted pride that belied the gruesome nature of his collection. He cherished these morbid trophies with a reverence that was both sickening and chilling.

"Perfection," he murmured, his voice barely more than a whisper. "Every lock I defeat brings me closer to mastery."

His gaze shifted from the glinting pendant to the blueprint spread out on the table. It was the layout of Olivia's home, a new challenge for him to conquer. She had recently moved to town, unaware of the danger she would soon face. He traced each corner of the blueprint with his finger, muttering under his breath as he planned his next "test" down to the smallest detail.

"Ah, the front door...a brand-new lock, just waiting to be picked," he observed, his voice tinged with anticipation. "Olivia, my dear, are you ready to face my challenge?"

He stared intently at one particular section of the blueprint – the newly installed door lock on Olivia's home. It seemed to trigger an unnerving sense of excitement within him, fueling his obsession even further.

"Will you rise to the occasion?" he pondered aloud. "Or will you crumble under the weight of your own vulnerability, like so many others before you?"

As he studied the blueprint, his fingers twitched involuntarily, itching for the tactile sensation of lockpicking tools in his hands. His heart raced with the thrill of the hunt, the prospect of another test looming ever closer.

"Only time will tell if you're worthy, Olivia," he whispered, his voice dripping with menace. "But rest assured, I'll be watching...and waiting."

With a cold determination etched upon his features, he returned his focus to the blueprint, refining his plans and ensuring every detail was accounted for. Nothing would be left to chance – not when the stakes were so high.

"Let the games begin."

With a sinister smile, he reached for a box labeled 'Olivia's Lock'. Carefully lifting the lid, his eyes gleamed as they fell upon the replica of Olivia's door lock. It was time to put his skills to the test.

"Time for a little practice," he murmured to himself, setting the lock on the workbench before him.

One by one, he methodically selected an array of different lock-picking tools from his collection, each chosen with purpose and precision. With practiced hands and unyielding focus, he began to pick the lock, his fingers dancing nimbly over the intricate mechanism.

"Almost there..." he muttered, beads of sweat forming on his brow as he worked.

Finally, with a satisfying click, the lock sprang open. A triumphant grin spread across his face as he reveled in the success of his practice session. The satisfaction in his eyes signaled his readiness to strike again, adding an eerie finality to his preparations.

"Olivia… you're next."

CHAPTER NINETEEN

Late afternoon sun filtered through the trees as Morgan drove down a winding country road, Derik beside her in the passenger seat. They were en route to meet the expert profiler, Steve Adams, who had agreed to help them with their case.

"Tell me more about this Steve guy," Morgan asked, her grip tightening on the steering wheel.

"Steve Adams was a top profiler with the Dallas PD before he retired," Derik explained, looking over at Morgan. "He's worked with the FBI on several cases, so I think he'll be a great asset to our investigation."

Morgan nodded, taking in the information. She couldn't shake the feeling that time was running out, and she hoped this profiler could provide some much-needed insight into the mind of the killer.

As they continued down the road, Morgan's thoughts drifted back to the victims they'd encountered thus far. She couldn't help but feel responsible for their deaths, as if she'd somehow failed them. But she was determined to bring the killer to justice – for their sake and for any potential future victims.

Morgan glanced over at him and offered a small smile, grateful for his support. Together, they would do everything in their power to stop the killer – no matter what it took.

The sun dipped below the horizon, casting a warm glow over the country road as Morgan guided their car around a bend. Her eyes flickered to the rearview mirror, catching sight of the ominous clouds that seemed to be following them – a reminder of the ever-present darkness threatening to engulf them.

"Is everything okay?" Derik asked, his voice gentle yet concerned.

Morgan hesitated for a moment, torn between wanting to confide in her partner and maintaining the strong façade she had built up over the years. But as she thought about the text message she'd received from Thomas about Skunk, her resolve crumbled. She needed to share this burden with someone she could trust.

"Actually, no," she admitted, gripping the steering wheel tighter. "I've been having these… nightmares lately. They're getting worse."

"Nightmares?" Derik echoed, his gaze fixed on her. "About what?"

"About the victims," she whispered, feeling the weight of their lost lives pressing down on her chest. "I see their faces, hear their screams. And I know it's not real, but I can't help feeling like I'm failing them somehow."

As she spoke, Morgan could see the understanding in Derik's eyes, the empathy that came from sharing a similar sense of responsibility. He reached over and placed a comforting hand on her arm, his touch warm and soothing.

"We'll find him, Morgan," he assured her, his voice steady and strong. "We won't let him hurt anyone else."

A sudden jolt of romantic tension filled the air as their hands brushed against each other, causing both of them to quickly pull back. The fleeting moment passed, replaced by a renewed determination to focus.

"Let's make sure we're prepared for our meeting with Steve," Derik suggested, tactfully steering the conversation away from their shared vulnerability. "The more we know, the better our chances of catching this guy."

Morgan nodded, grateful for Derik's support and his ability to keep them focused on the mission. As they continued down the road towards their meeting with the profiler, she felt a flicker of hope – hope that together, they would finally bring an end to the killer's deadly game.

The quaint cottage loomed ahead, its warm glow cutting through the twilight as Morgan parked the car. A fragrant scent of roses and lavender filled the air, a stark contrast to the grim purpose that had brought them here. She glanced at Derik, taking a steadying breath before they stepped out into the cool evening.

"Here goes nothing," she murmured, her voice barely audible above the whispering breeze.

As they approached the door, it swung open to reveal a tall, wiry man in his sixties with a shock of white hair and piercing blue eyes. Steve Adams greeted them with a firm handshake, his grip strong despite his age, evidence of a long career spent wrestling criminals into submission.

"Agent Cross, Agent Greene, welcome," he said, his voice gravelly and tinged with a hint of Texas drawl. "I've heard about your case, and I'm eager to help you catch this monster."

Morgan managed a tight smile, grateful for his willingness to assist, yet acutely aware of the dwindling time they had to stop the killer from striking again.

"Thank you for agreeing to meet with us, Mr. Adams," she replied, following him inside the cozy living room.

The walls were lined with an impressive array of memorabilia from Steve's time on the force – badges, commendations, and newspaper clippings of high-profile cases he'd helped solve. Morgan's gaze lingered on a faded photograph of Steve with a group of fellow officers, all grinning proudly after a successful operation. She couldn't help but wonder if her father had ever stood alongside colleagues like these, secretly working undercover for the FBI.

Shaking off the distracting thought, she focused on Steve as he settled into a worn leather armchair, gesturing for them to do the same.

"Let's get down to business," he said, his eyes sharp and alert. "What have you discovered so far, and where do you think we should start looking?"

Morgan passed him the cryptic, coded letter they'd received from the killer. "So far, no one has been able to crack what this means. Any chance you can make it out?"

Steve took the letter from her, his brows furrowing as he read the haphazardly scrawled words. "Well, I reckon it's not something we can decipher easily, but I've handled some pretty tricky ciphers in my time. I'll do what I can."

The retired profiler's words were a beacon of tentative hope in their otherwise grim reality. Morgan found herself holding her breath as Steve started to mumble, tracing the letters with a finger and jotting down notes on a pad of paper.

Time seemed to stretch on as they watched Steve work, the room filled with an anticipation that sat heavy on their chests. Morgan cast a side glance at Derik, who was bouncing his leg up and down nervously.

"You okay?" she whispered, noticing how his Adam's apple bobbed as he swallowed hard.

"I just... I want this to be over," he admitted quietly, his gaze focused on Steve. "I want us to catch this guy."

Morgan nodded in agreement, her grip tightening around the edge of her seat. "We will," she reassured him, trying to sound more confident than she felt. "We have to."

A sudden clearing of throat interrupted their whispered conversation. They turned back to Steve, who was now leaning back in his chair, rubbing at his temples.

"This cipher... it's unlike anything I've seen before," he confessed, tossing the notepad onto the coffee table in front of him. "But there's a pattern...a repetition of certain letters and symbols."

"Do you think you can break it?" Derik asked hopefully, but Steve only offered a tired shrug.

"I can. But you're gonna have to give me a minute. What else do we know about this guy?"

"Locks," Morgan replied, her voice steady as she explained their findings. "We believe the killer is an expert lock-picker, using his skill to infiltrate his victims' homes."

Steve nodded thoughtfully, his brow furrowing as he considered the implications. "Interesting," he mused. "I've come across a few cases like that in my time – killers who derive some twisted satisfaction from overcoming security measures. It's all about control, proving they can outsmart their prey. This cipher could be like a lock too... or a key."

The room lapsed into silence as they pondered Steve's words. It was a new perspective, one that hadn't occurred to Morgan or Derik before. Could the coded messages be part of the killer's twisted sense of superiority? A coded lock only he could open?

"It fits," Derik conceded, his knuckles white against the armrest of his chair. "We've found no signs of forced entry in all the crime scenes. All victims were seemingly unaware until..."

"Until it was too late," Morgan finished for him, her voice hollow. Steve nodded grimly, his gaze darkening.

He turned his eyes back to the letter, frowning.

"Alright," he said, taking a deep breath. "I think I've got an alternate approach we can try. Let's not think of it just as a random set of letters, but rather... keys. It might be something more significant, a puzzle that requires a specific tool to decode."

Steve reached for a drawer in the nearby wooden table and pulled out an antique-looking device. It was about the size of a typewriter, with numerous dials and levers.

"This," he explained, "is an Enigma machine used during World War II to encrypt and decrypt messages. I've been collecting and studying these machines for years."

Morgan stared at the contraption in awe, and even Derik seemed momentarily distracted by it. It was a relic of a different time, a threat long past, yet here it was being brought into their grim present.

"Are you suggesting..." Morgan's voice trailed off as she caught on to Steve's train of thought.

"That our killer is using an old encryption method? Possibly," Steve confirmed, his fingers hovering over the keys of the Enigma machine. "Just because it's old doesn't mean it's not effective."

"But wouldn't we need... I don't know, an original code book or something?" Derik questioned, his brow furrowed in confusion.

"Usually, yes," Steve replied, his hands moving over the machine with practiced ease. "But I've spent a good part of my life studying these machines and their codes. I won't make any promises, but there's a chance I can crack it without a code book."

With that, he started to input the scrambled letters from the note into the machine, his fingers dancing over the keys. The room was filled with the soft clacking of machinery and a tension so palpable it was like another entity in itself.

Morgan and Derik exchanged apprehensive glances as they watched Steve work. The profiler's face was illuminated by the dim light of the desk lamp, his furrowed brow reflecting his concentration. His eyes flickered as he deciphered the pattern behind the seemingly random letters.

A long while passed, with only the rhythmic tapping of keys echoing in the silence. Morgan found herself unconsciously measuring out seconds in her head, each one dragging longer than the last. Derik had stopped bouncing his leg - every ounce of his attention was now fixated on Steve.

Suddenly, Steve's fingers stilled. He leaned back in his chair and stared at the decoded message that spilled out of the Enigma machine.

"Well?" Derik asked after a moment, breaking the silence.

"It says... family," Steve said, confusion crossing his brow.

Morgan froze. "Family?" She echoed, the word heavy with implications.

Steve nodded, his eyes scanning the decoded message again. "Yes, it just says 'family'. Nothing more."

Derik's brow furrowed deeply, his mind racing. "Could it be a hint to the next victim? Or maybe it refers to the killer's motive?"

"Or a cryptic signature," Steve suggested. "I'm not sure what it means."

Family. Was that the key? Or was it random chaos?

"Tell me more about these lock-obsessed killers," Morgan asked, her eyes scanning the bookshelves that lined Steve's office walls. The room was dimly lit, casting shadows over countless books and souvenirs from his days with the force.

Steve leaned back in his armchair, fingers tapping against the armrest as he delved into his wealth of knowledge. "Well, for one thing, it's not just about breaking into someone's home. It's about conquering their sense of security. Defeating a lock is like solving a puzzle – only this time, the prize is control over another person's life."

"Control," Morgan echoed, trying to wrap her mind around this twisted thought process. Derik sat next to her, taking notes on every detail, his green eyes flicking between Steve and the notepad.

"Exactly." Steve continued, his voice heavy with experience. "In many cases, these individuals have experienced some form of confinement or abandonment in their childhood. This obsession with locks can be seen as a way of regaining power over their own lives – albeit in a very twisted manner."

Morgan felt a shiver run down her spine at the thought of the killer's motivations being rooted in such dark, personal experiences. She focused on Steve's words, determined to absorb every piece of information that could help them catch him.

"Is there anything specific we should look for when examining crime scenes?" Derik asked, his pen poised above the paper.

"Pay close attention to the locks themselves," Steve advised. "These killers take pride in their work; they're not likely to leave any obvious signs of tampering. Look for subtle clues – scratches, marks, anything that might indicate the lock was picked."

"Thank you, Mr. Adams," Morgan said, her gaze intense as she locked eyes with the profiler. "This has been incredibly helpful. We'll use your insights to narrow down our search and try to prevent any more deaths. As for the 'family' clue... part of me is starting to wonder if I need to be looking deeper into the victims' families."

"Perhaps," Steve replied, leaning back into his chair, his fingers absently tracing the edges of the Enigma machine. "But why 'family'? Is it because they share a common trait? Or perhaps the killer is related to one of them?" He paused, lost in thought. "Or could it be that the family is a group of people we haven't considered yet?"

Morgan’s mind whirled with possibilities. The word 'family' now held a sinister undertone, but she was determined to find out what it meant.

CHAPTER TWENTY

Back at the hotel, Morgan sat at the small desk in their room, her laptop casting a ghostly glow on her face. She scrolled through the FBI database, searching for any information that could help them pinpoint the killer. With each click, her determination grew, fueled by the desire to put an end to this nightmare. She wondered what the message left in the strange letter really meant—if "family" was the key to solving all of this, somehow.

Determined to leave no stone unturned, Morgan turned her attention to Jennifer's case files – the first victim whose murder had gone unsolved for years. She studied the documents with renewed focus, searching for any clue they might have missed back then. Surely, there had to be a reason why Jennifer had been targeted, and it couldn't be mere chance.

Morgan's fingers tapped impatiently on the desk as she scanned the search results for Jennifer's ex-husband, George Bannon. She found an address and phone number listed in Dallas – he had never remarried. Morgan hesitated for a moment, wondering if it was worth pursuing. But with no other leads at hand, she decided to give him a call.

"Hello?" a gruff voice answered on the other end of the line.

"Hi, is this George Bannon?" Morgan asked, her heart pounding in her chest.

"Who's asking?"

"My name is Morgan Cross. I'm an FBI agent investigating the murder of your ex-wife, Jennifer." Morgan's words hung heavy between them, the silence a palpable weight before George finally spoke again.

"Jennifer? It's been so long… What do you want to know?"

"Thank you for agreeing to talk to me," Morgan said, trying to sound empathetic. "I understand this may be difficult for you, but any information you can provide could help us solve her case."

George sighed. "Yeah, alright. We divorced years ago, but Jennifer… she was the love of my life. I never got over her."

Morgan nodded, even though George couldn't see her. "I'm sorry for your loss. Do you remember anything about the time leading up to her murder? Did she ever mention anyone being suspicious or stalking her?"

"No, nothing like that," George replied, his voice heavy with sorrow. "She moved to Charlesberg to start fresh after the divorce. I never thought something like this would happen."

"Did she ever have trouble with her locks? Or did she mention anyone who might have had access to her house?" Morgan probed, hoping to find some connection to their current investigation.

"Locks?" George paused, considering the question. "No, not that I can remember. Why do you ask?"

"Because we believe the same person who killed Jennifer has recently murdered two other women in Charlesberg. The killer seems to have an obsession with locks, and we're trying to find any possible connections."

"Jesus," George whispered, the shock palpable in his voice. "I can't believe this is happening again."

"Neither can we." Morgan hesitated, then continued, "We think the killer might be an expert lock-picker. Does that ring any bells for you?"

There was a pause on the other end of the line, and Morgan could almost picture George racking his brain for any relevant memories. Finally, he spoke up. "You know, there was a guy I used to know back when Jennifer and I were still together. He was great at picking locks, but... well, he was a bit of a drunk asshole, if I'm being honest. I stopped talking to him after a while."

"Did you ever get the sense that he had a thing for Jennifer?" Morgan asked, her heart pounding in her chest.

"Maybe. He always seemed a little too interested in her, and it made me uncomfortable," George admitted. "But that was years ago. I haven't seen or heard from him in ages."

"Can you tell me his name?" Morgan inquired, gripping her phone tighter as if it could somehow convey the urgency of their situation to George.

"His name was..." George paused for a moment, as if trying to recall a distant memory. "Gregory Haus."

"Where does he live?" Morgan asked, her voice tense with anticipation.

"Last I heard, Gregory was living in his parents' old house after they passed away," George said. "I'm not sure of the exact address, but it's somewhere in Charlesberg."

"Thank you, George," Morgan replied, her mind racing as she processed the lead. "You've been a great help."

"Anything to catch that monster," George replied solemnly before hanging up.

Morgan set her phone down on the desk, her thoughts swirling like a tornado. As she mulled over the new information, Derik walked into the room, carrying bags of takeout food. The smell of greasy burgers and fries filled the air, momentarily distracting Morgan from the case.

"Hey, I got us some dinner," Derik said, placing the bags on the table. He noticed the intense expression on Morgan's face and furrowed his brow. "Everything okay?"

"Derik," Morgan said abruptly, standing up and facing him, her dark eyes filled with determination. "We have a new suspect, and this one might be the real killer."

"Really? Who is it?" Derik asked, his green eyes widening with surprise as he took in Morgan's serious demeanor.

"His name is Gregory Haus," she answered, the name feeling heavy on her tongue. "He's an expert lock-picker, and according to Jennifer's ex-husband, he had a thing for her. He's in his fifties now and works as a groundskeeper."

"Interesting," Derik mused, his mind already shifting gears to focus on this new lead. "What's our next move, then?"

"First, we need to find out where Gregory lives," Morgan said. Her fingers tapped against the desk, betraying her impatience. "Then, we pay him a visit and see what he knows."

"Sounds like a plan," Derik agreed, his voice steady and professional. "We should eat first, though. We'll need our energy for whatever comes next."

Morgan nodded reluctantly, knowing Derik was right, but her appetite had all but vanished in the face of their latest revelation. As they sat down to eat their rapidly cooling dinner, she couldn't help but wonder if they were finally on the verge of catching the vicious killer who had eluded them for so long.

"Let's hope this lead pans out," Morgan thought grimly, taking a bite of her burger with little enthusiasm. The sooner they could put an end to this nightmare, the better.

CHAPTER TWENTY ONE

The night was dark and heavy as Morgan and Derik pulled up to the old farmhouse. Its decaying exterior seemed to hide a world of secrets within its walls, shrouded in darkness. Shadows danced in the moonlight, casting eerie silhouettes of gnarled trees and broken fences across the barren landscape. The distant rustle of dried leaves and the haunting hoot of an owl created an unsettling atmosphere that sent a chill down Morgan's spine.

"Something doesn't feel right," she muttered under her breath, as they slowly approached the seemingly abandoned house. Her tattoos seemed to shift and twist in the dim light, a constant reminder of her time in prison and the hardships she had endured.

Derik nodded in agreement. "I know what you mean," he whispered back. His sharply dressed figure stood in stark contrast to the disheveled surroundings, though the shadows under his eyes betrayed his exhaustion.

They walked up to the house, and Morgan's heart thrummed in her chest. This was where Gregory Haus lived? Seeing the state of the area made her feel even more so like he had something to hide. But was he the one who'd been murdering those women?

Guess we should knock, Morgan thought, approaching the porch. A light clicked on, startling her for a moment.

"Can I help you?"

A sudden, gruff voice cut into the night air, causing Morgan's hair to stand on end. She and Derik turned to face a figure who was emerging from the shadows around the side of the house, wiping his hands on a towel. The man's overalls were stained and his hair unkempt, giving him an air of menace that set Morgan's heart racing.

Gregory Haus.

"Who are you?" Gregory asked gruffly, squinting at the two agents.

Morgan and Derik quickly produced their badges, identifying themselves as FBI agents. "Morgan Cross, FBI," Morgan said, her voice steady and authoritative. "And this is my partner, Derik Greene."

Gregory eyed them warily, his gaze lingering on Morgan's tattoos for a moment before returning to her face. He seemed to weigh their presence, calculating his options. Morgan could feel the tension in the air, and she knew that whatever secrets this old farmhouse held, they were on the verge of uncovering them.

"Can we talk inside?" Morgan asked, her eyes narrowing as she scrutinized Gregory's face, searching for any sign of deception.

"Not now," he replied curtly, crossing his arms defensively. “I’m awfully busy, and it’s a mess inside.” The shadows of the moonlit night seemed to cling to him, making him appear all the more sinister. His reluctance to let them into his home only served to heighten Morgan's suspicions.

"Fine," Morgan said, a steely edge in her voice. "We'll talk out here." She glanced at Derik, who gave her a subtle nod of agreement.

Morgan couldn't help but notice how Gregory's nervous eyes kept darting towards a closed door in an obscure corner on the outside of the house. What was going on behind that door? What was he hiding? Her instincts told her that the answer to those questions could be vital to their investigation.

"Gregory," she said, trying to maintain a calm tone despite the growing unease gnawing at her insides, "we're investigating the death of Jennifer Stacy. We understand you knew her. Can you tell us about your connection to her?"

"Jennifer?" Gregory hesitated for a moment, his gaze flicking back towards the mysterious door before returning to meet Morgan's. "Yeah, I knew her. She was my old friend's ex-wife. But what's that got to do with me?"

"Did you ever visit her?" Derik interjected, studying Gregory's face intently, trying to discern any hint of guilt or fear.

"Maybe once or twice," Gregory replied, shrugging his shoulders nonchalantly. "But like I said, she was my friend's ex. We weren't close."

Morgan noted the flicker of unease cross his face as he spoke, her intuition kicking in. She decided to push further, "When was the last time you saw her, Mr. Haus?"

Gregory's brows furrowed, his eyes betraying a fleeting hint of panic. "That would have been...years ago. I don't remember the exact date."

Once more, he glanced at the cellar door at the side of the house. Morgan's eyes narrowed further, focusing on the door that seemed to hold such importance for Gregory. Her gut told her that there was something significant hidden behind it, and she was determined to find out what. The truth was tantalizingly close, and she would stop at nothing to uncover it.

"Gregory," she began, her voice low and measured, "what's behind that door you keep glancing at?"

"Oh, that old thing? Just the old meat cellar. Nothing to see there."

The dismissive tone of Gregory's reply didn't sit well with Morgan. In her experience, it was the casual dismissals that often hid the most important clues.

"Would you mind if we took a look inside?" She asked, her eyes never leaving his face.

Gregory's reaction was immediate and telling. His face blanched, and he took a half step backward, bumping into the wall of the house as he did so.

"I, uh... I can't let you do that without a warrant." He stammered out the words in a rush, avoiding eye contact.

"That's not exactly necessary," Derik interjected smoothly, stepping forward. "Unless there's something to hide."

"No, but I know my rights," Gregory shot back. "I don't have to show you into anything."

Morgan shared a glance with Derik, the unspoken agreement clear between them: they needed to see what lay beyond the door. They couldn't afford to leave any stone unturned in their pursuit for justice, no matter how dark and twisted the path may become.

"Gregory, I'm going to need you to let us take a look in that cellar," Morgan insisted, her voice firm but steady. "If you have nothing to hide in there, then it shouldn't be an issue."

The air around them seemed to thicken with tension as she locked eyes with the nervous man.

"Fine," he conceded reluctantly, wiping his hands on his overalls again. "But there's really nothing in there."

Morgan nodded and gestured for him to lead the way. As they walked towards the cellar door, she couldn't help but notice the stiffness in Gregory's movements, the way his fingers twitched at his sides. Her instincts screamed that something was wrong, and the tightness in her chest only grew stronger.

"Here," Gregory said as they reached the door, his voice strained. He fumbled with the padlock, unlocking it with trembling hands. Morgan watched him closely, feeling Derik's presence beside her like a reassuring anchor.

In an instant, everything shifted. Gregory's hand shot out towards a nearby shelf, and Morgan's heart plummeted as she recognized the shape of a shotgun resting there.

Time seemed to slow as Gregory grabbed the weapon, lifting it with surprising speed.

"Derik, move!" Morgan shouted, her voice raw with urgency. She lunged towards her partner, shoving him out of the way just as the shotgun roared to life. The blast echoed through the night air, and Morgan felt the heat of the pellets as they whizzed past her cheek, narrowly missing both agents.

"Damn it, Gregory!" Derik yelled from behind the cover of a nearby tree, his voice tight with anger and fear. His green eyes met Morgan's, the intensity of their shared adrenaline coursing through them like electric current.

Morgan's mind raced, searching for a way to defuse the situation without further violence. But as she stared at the defiant figure of Gregory Haus, shotgun in hand and a wild look in his eyes, she knew that they had crossed a line from which there was no turning back. And as her fingers tightened around the grip of her own weapon, she couldn't help but wonder what dark secrets lay hidden within that cellar – secrets worth killing for.

"Gregory, put the gun down!" she demanded, her voice wavering only slightly. She could feel the weight of Derik's concern beside her, but she refused to let it distract her. This was her fight to finish, and she would see it through to the bitter end.

A pounding heartbeat filled Morgan's ears, drowning out the distant hooting of an owl as she pressed her back against the rough wooden surface of the old shed. Derik crouched beside her, his own gun drawn and held steady in his shaking hands. The moon cast ghostly shadows across their faces as they exchanged tense glances, each silently acknowledging the gravity of the situation unfolding before them.

"Stay back!" Gregory warned, a sneer playing at the corners of his lips as he leveled the shotgun at them. "I ain't got nothin' to hide."

"Really?" Morgan hissed through gritted teeth. "Then why are you pointing that gun at us, Gregory?"

"Y'all have no right to be here," he spat, his grip on the shotgun tightening. "Now get off my property!"

Morgan's chest tightened as another shot rang out, the sound echoing through the night like the crack of a whip. Instinct took over, and she ducked behind the shed just as a hail of splinters erupted from the decaying wood where the bullet had struck. Beside her, Derik let out a string of curses before returning fire, his aim steady even as his face betrayed his fear.

This wasn't what they had signed up for, but there was no turning back now.

Morgan knew that whatever secrets Gregory was hiding in that cellar were worth fighting for. She could feel it in her bones.

"Derik," she whispered, her voice barely audible over the ringing in their ears from the gunfire, "I'm going to make a run for the house. Cover me."

Derik met her gaze, his eyes wide. "Morgan," he began, shaking his head adamantly. But the look in her eyes stopped him mid-sentence. He knew there was no point in arguing with her. Morgan was as stubborn as they come, and when she set her mind to something, there was no stopping her.

She took a deep breath, mentally preparing herself for the sprint. She had one shot at this — Gregory's attention would be split between shooting at Derik and aiming at her.

"Now!" She yelled, and Derik let loose a volley of shots toward Gregory's position. Taking advantage of the distraction, Morgan lunged from behind the shed and made a beeline for the house.

Her heart pounded in her chest like a drum as she ran across the moonlit yard. Each step felt heavy and slow, as if she were running through molasses. Behind her, she could hear Derik continuing to fire at Gregory, keeping him distracted.

As she neared the porch steps, a sudden blast ricocheted off the wooden railing next to her, giving her pause. But she didn't dare stop; she powered through, propelling herself up the steps and through the front door.

Once inside, she slammed the door shut and pressed her back against it, gasping for breath. Sweat trickled down her face as her chest heaved from the adrenaline coursing through her veins. A quick scan of the room revealed nothing out of place, but she knew better than to take things at face value. Drawing her gun, she moved swiftly through what seemed to be a well-lived-in house. The scent of old books and slightly burnt coffee filled her nostrils as she carefully navigated through the dimly lit rooms.

Outside, Derik was still exchanging fire with Gregory, using their car as cover.

"Morgan?!" Derik's voice crackled through her earpiece, his tone worried yet trying to stay composed. "Are you in?"

"I'm in," she responded quietly, her voice steady though her heart was pounding in her chest. "Don't die out there, Greene," she said. "I'm gonna sneak out the back and get him."

"Stay alive, Cross," Derik shot back, his voice clipped and tense.

Squaring her shoulders, Morgan moved through the house with a silent grace that came from years of experience. She knew she had to move quickly, but she also knew that one wrong step could be fatal. Every creaking floorboard, every flicker of shadow made her heart pound against her ribcage like a war drum.

Morgan's earpiece crackled in her ear with Derik's voice, saying, "Cross, I've lost eyes on him--get out of there!"

The back door was just a few steps away when she heard the ominous click of a shotgun being loaded. "Not so fast, agent," a drawling voice whispered from the darkness.

Morgan froze. Gregory stood in the doorframe of what seemed to be a study, the pale moonlight highlighting the sweat on his brow and the wild desperation in his eyes. His twitchy finger rested on the shotgun's trigger while he pointed at her with a shaky hand.

"Looks like you've reached the end of your road, girl," Gregory said, his lips curling into a cruel sneer.

There was no escape now, Morgan realized. The only way out was back where she'd come from, but with Gregory blocking her path, that wasn't an option. She had to think fast.

"Gregory," she started, her voice steady even as her heart pounded in her chest. "You don't have to do this."

His smile didn't falter. "Oh, I think I do."

The next few moments were a blur. She heard the deafening roar of the shotgun echoing off the walls of the house, felt the rush of adrenaline as she dove for cover behind a heavy wooden desk - just in time to avoid getting blown apart by a hailstorm of lead.

Damn it, he's aiming to kill, Morgan thought as she huddled behind her makeshift cover. She felt a sudden surge of anger. She couldn't die here, not like this.

Without another thought, she drew her gun and jumped out of cover, ready to take the shot.

But as she did, Gregory pointed his shotgun right at her.

Then, another loud bang resounded through the house.

CHAPTER TWENTY TWO

Morgan held her breath as the gunshot rang out in her ears.

Time seemed to slow. For a moment, she wondered if Gregory had fired a blast right at her, and she'd been hit.

But the pain never came.

As Morgan's eyes adjusted to the darkness, she heard the thud of a body dropping. It was then she realized that Derik was standing right there, gun drawn and pointed right at Gregory's now immobile body.

His hands were steady, his eyes cold and hard with resolve. He seemed to have appeared out of nowhere, stepping through the shadows like a ghost materializing out of thin air.

"Morgan," he called out, lowering his gun and rushing toward her. "You okay?"

"Yeah," she managed to cough out, slowly rising from behind the desk, her own gun still clutched tightly in her hand. She stared at Gregory's body lying sprawled out on the floor, a pool of red seeping across the wooden floorboards beneath him. It was over.

Derik reached her side, quickly checking her over for injuries. His face was a mask of worry even as relief washed over him. "You scared the hell out of me, Cross."

She smirked at him, her breaths still ragged from adrenaline. "You should know by now I don't frighten easily, Greene."

He let out a breathy laugh, shaking his head in disbelief. "Yeah, I'm beginning to see that."

An eerie silence settled over them as the reality of what happened sank in. They had come so dangerously close to losing this fight. But they made it. Morgan glanced at the lifeless body lying a few feet away from them. It never felt good to lose a suspect in this way--to take a life--but sometimes, in this job, it was necessary.

Morgan and Derik cautiously approached Gregory's form, which was now spilling blood all over the hardwood. Derik bent down to check Gregory's pulse, his fingers pressing firmly against the man's neck.

"Is he..." Morgan began, her voice barely above a whisper.

"Dead," Derik confirmed gravely. The reality of their actions settled heavily upon them. But the question that loomed largest in their minds was what secret lay hidden within Gregory's cellar, a secret worth dying for.

"Let's find out what he was hiding," Morgan said.

***

The moon peeked out from behind scudding clouds, casting a pale glow on the weathered exterior of the farmhouse. Morgan and Derik exchanged a tense glance before turning their attention to the cellar door. The eerie stillness that surrounded them seemed to press in from all sides, urging them to proceed with caution.

"Ready?" Derik asked quietly, his green eyes dark with apprehension.

"Always," Morgan replied, her voice steady despite the rapid beating of her heart. The tattoos that adorned her arms were barely visible under the dim moonlight, but she knew they served as a constant reminder of the strength she had gleaned from her own past, from her time in prison.

Derik's hand rested on the iron latch, a fine tremor betraying his unease. He drew a deep breath and pulled it open, the hinges groaning in protest. A musty odor wafted out, assaulting their senses and causing them both to wrinkle their noses in distaste.

As they peered into the gloom, the scene that awaited them sent shivers down their spines. Concrete walls glistened with moisture, while flickering bulbs cast eerie shadows that danced across the space like malevolent spirits. The distant sound of dripping water echoed through the confined area, amplifying the chilling atmosphere.

"God, what is this place?" Derik muttered, his voice barely audible.

"I don't know," Morgan murmured, her dark eyes scanning the unsettling surroundings. "But whatever Gregory was hiding down here, it has to be important."

"Or dangerous," Derik added grimly, stepping cautiously onto the damp steps that led into the cellar. Morgan followed, her grip tightening around her gun as they descended.

"Stay close," she instructed, her mind racing with thoughts of what could possibly be worth killing for. Was it evidence of another crime? Or something even more sinister? Whatever it was, they had to discover the truth.

"Right behind you, Morgan," Derik acknowledged, his voice strained as they carefully navigated their way through the darkness, determined to uncover the secret that had been buried beneath the farmhouse.

As the pair reached the bottom of the creaky stairs, the full extent of the horror became apparent. The basement was divided into a series of small, makeshift cells, each one imprisoning a fear-stricken young woman who had been bound and gagged. Their eyes widened in terror and hope as they caught sight of Morgan and Derik.

"Jesus Christ," Derik breathed, recoiling at the sight. His face paled under the dim light, horror etched into his features.

Morgan felt her blood run cold, a wave of revulsion washing over her. She had seen some gruesome things in her time on the job, but this was something else entirely.

"Derik. Call it in," she ordered, trying to keep her voice steady. Her eyes roved over the scared women, their bodies trembling with fear, their eyes pleading for salvation. To think that Gregory had been harboring such a dark secret was enough to make bile rise in her throat.

Derik nodded wordlessly, pulling out his radio and quickly reporting their grim find back to headquarters. Meanwhile, Morgan cautiously approached one of the cells, careful not to startle the occupant.

"Hey," she began in a soft tone. "We're with the FBI. We're here to help you."

As she said the words, she could see a glimmer of hope spark in the girl's wide eyes. Though still terrified, there was a sense of relief that seemed to wash over her.

"Please… help us," the girl sobbed through her gag, her eyes pleading with Morgan. "He said he'd kill us if anyone found us…"

"Nobody's going to hurt you anymore," Morgan vowed, carefully removing the filthy cloth from the girl's mouth before moving on to untie her wrists. "My name is Morgan, and my partner Derik is calling for help right now. We won't leave until all of you are safe, I promise."

"Th-thank you," the girl stammered, tears streaming down her face as Morgan helped her to her feet. "I thought we were going to die down here…"

"Help is on the way," Derik called over from where he stood by the stairs, having just hung up from his call. "They'll be here soon."

"Good," Morgan replied, her jaw clenched in determination as she moved on to the next captive, working to free her. "We need to get them out of this hellhole as soon as possible."

"Whatever you need, Morgan," Derik agreed, his eyes sweeping the horrors that surrounded them with a mixture of disgust and pity. "I'm here for you."

"I know," she replied softly, her gaze meeting his for a moment as she continued to work. "Thank you, Derik."

As the minutes ticked by and the captives were freed one by one, Morgan couldn't help but feel a sense of overwhelming relief and gratitude that they had discovered this nightmare in time. But even as she focused on the task at hand, her thoughts kept straying back to the case that had brought them here – the killer they were chasing after.

"Derik," she murmured as she worked, her voice barely audible above the quiet sobs and whispers of the girls around them. "This isn't our guy. This isn't the killer we're after. Something's not right."

"Let's focus on getting these girls to safety first," he replied, his voice equally hushed. "We'll figure out the rest later. Right now, they need us."

Morgan nodded, knowing he was right. They had come face-to-face with evil tonight, and it was their duty to rescue the innocent from its clutches. But as Morgan comforted another sobbing girl, a nagging feeling gnawed at the back of her mind, telling her that their work was far from over.

CHAPTER TWENTY THREE

The rescued victims' tear-streaked faces haunted Morgan's thoughts as she sat in her office at the FBI headquarters. She couldn't shake the feeling that, although they had saved these girls, Gregory's methods didn't match the killer they were after. There was a sickening sense of unease lodged deep within her chest.

"Gregory's MO is different," she muttered to herself, staring blankly at the paperwork on her desk. "It doesn't add up."

She rubbed her temples, mentally retracing their steps in the investigation. The hooting of an owl outside her window seemed to echo the same questions that plagued her mind. What did she miss? Why did it feel like there was still a piece of the puzzle missing?

A sudden knock on the door startled her. Assistant Director Mueller's imposing figure filled the doorway as he poked his head in, his eyes scanning the office before landing on Morgan. "Agent Cross," he said gruffly. "How are you holding up? Finding all those victims in that man's cellar must have been awful."

She looked up at him, her gaze steady. "It was, sir. But I can't help but feel like Gregory's MO doesn't fit the profile for our killer. I think he's still out there."

Mueller furrowed his brow, crossing his arms over his chest. "Wasn't Gregory known to be a lockpick and acquainted with the first victim? Plus, he was obviously a deranged criminal; seems like an open and shut case."

As he spoke, Morgan couldn't help but notice the way his tone shifted, almost as if he wanted her to drop her suspicions. She clenched her jaw, irritation prickling beneath her skin. "I disagree, sir. The MO is far too different. Our killer has been meticulous—leaving no evidence, no witnesses. Gregory's actions were erratic and desperate."

Her words hung in the air, the tension between them palpable. Mueller's eyes narrowed, a flicker of doubt registering in his expression. After a brief pause, he sighed. "Regardless of whether he's our main suspect or not, you did a good thing by saving those women in the cellar," Mueller reminded her, his voice taking on a gentler tone.

"Thank you, sir." Morgan managed a small smile as he left her office.

Alone with her thoughts, she glanced at the clock on her wall. Almost nine p.m. Her fingers drummed on her desk, a distant ache settling in her chest. She couldn't shake the nagging feeling that something was missed. If she left now, she could get to Charlesberg by 9:30 if traffic permitted.

Decision made, Morgan grabbed her coat and headed out into the night.

***

The cold air stung Morgan's cheeks as she stepped out of her car, the world around her shrouded in darkness. She stood outside Lucy's apartment building, lit only by the faint glow of a flickering streetlight. The first-floor apartment remained sealed off, a crime scene frozen in time.

Morgan hesitated a moment before pushing open the door, steeling herself for what lay within. As she stepped inside, a chill ran down her spine. The bloodstain on the carpet—where Lucy's body once laid—served as a stark reminder of the life that was brutally taken.

"Damn it, Lucy. What am I missing?" She muttered under her breath, her eyes scanning the room for any overlooked clues. Her heart ached with the weight of responsibility; she needed to find answers, to bring justice to those who had been taken too soon.

As she moved through the apartment, each step carried the heavy burden of her determination. This was personal for Morgan, and she refused to let the killer slip through her fingers.

Morgan’s footsteps echoed through the empty apartment as she ventured further in, her eyes scanning every corner for potential clues. The air felt heavy, suffocating her with the memories of Lucy's tragic end. Unsure of what she was searching for, she pressed on, driven by determination.

The kitchen appeared untouched, a relic of normalcy amid the chaos that had unfolded. Fliers cluttered the countertops, a testament to Lucy's recent move. Morgan's fingers traced over the paper edges, her thoughts racing as she sought meaning within the mundane.

"Maybe..." She mumbled to herself, her gaze catching an ad for a realtor group. Folding it carefully, she tucked it away in her pocket, a small seed of hope taking root in her mind.

***

Back at the hotel, the room was awash in the blue glow of her laptop screen. Morgan sat at the edge of the bed, her focus unwavering as she delved into her investigation. Derik's belongings were strewn across the room, a reminder of his absence. She'd tried calling him several times, but he hadn't answered.

"Where are you, Derik?" she muttered, her frustration mounting. But time was slipping away, and she couldn't afford to wait any longer.

Her fingers danced across the keyboard, a symphony of clicks and clacks as she pulled up everything she could find on the realtor group from the flier. Adrenaline coursed through her veins, fueling her tireless pursuit for answers.

"Come on, don't let me down," she thought, her eyes narrowing in concentration. The room seemed to fade away around her as she dove deeper into the digital world, determined to uncover the truth hidden beneath the surface.

Morgan's fingers hovered over the keyboard, her thoughts racing as she searched for information on the realtor group she'd found in Lucy's apartment. The shadows in the room seemed to deepen, pressing in on her as if trying to stifle her resolve, but she refused to let them win.

In the cold glow of her laptop screen, Morgan discovered that the company Lucy had dealt with didn't even appear to exist. Her heart hammered in her chest, the implications looming larger with each passing second. Both previous victims had been in the process of selling properties and moving into new ones. Could this realtor group be involved somehow?

"Damn it, Derik, where are you?" The words escaped her lips in a frustrated hiss, but there was no response. She couldn't afford to wait any longer; she needed to keep digging.

Curious, Morgan opened Sarah's file, searching for the name of the realtor she had been working with. Her brow furrowed in puzzlement when all she could find was a mention of a private sale. "What are you hiding, Sarah?" she murmured, her eyes scanning the file for any other clues.

With a growing sense of unease, Morgan delved further back, pulling up Jennifer's file. Her heart skipped a beat as she found the name of Jennifer's realtor: Ethan Snider. A lead at last. She leaned back in her chair, rubbing her tattooed arms, the inked images a testament to her past struggles.

"Who are you, Ethan Snider?" she mused, her voice barely audible in the stillness of the hotel room. Would he be the key to unlocking the mystery that surrounded these women and their deaths?

Morgan shook her head, dispelling the fog of doubt that had begun to cloud her thoughts. She needed to focus, to find the connection between these victims and this mysterious realtor. With renewed determination, she set her jaw and dove back into her investigation, each click of the keyboard a step toward uncovering the truth.

"Time to put the pieces together," she thought, her eyes narrowing as she hunted for answers in the digital abyss before her. And somewhere, hidden within the tangle of data, lay the truth she sought so desperately - the truth that would lead her to justice for Lucy, Sarah, and Jennifer.

A few clicks later, and she found herself looking at Ethan Snider's employment history. Her eyes narrowed as she read the information on the screen.

Real estate agent in Charlesberg, terminated by Homes On Us, she thought, committing the details to memory. "But no further record of employment after that." She leaned back in her chair, her tattooed fingers drumming on the edge of the hotel desk. If Ethan had been posing as a realtor to gain access to these women's homes, it would certainly explain how the killer could havc made keys to their locks.

Let's see what else the FBI database has on Mr. Snider, she said to herself, her fingers flying across the keyboard. As the sparse information loaded onto the screen, she felt a shiver of anticipation run down her spine.

"An address on file, but no criminal record," she read aloud, her voice tinged with frustration. It wasn't much, but it was a start. Morgan glanced at her watch, noting the time. Derik still hadn't answered his phone, and every second she spent waiting for him was another second the killer could slip through her fingers.

Morgan stood in the dimly lit hotel room, her heart pounding as she tried to call Derik one more time. The phone rang unanswered, the silence feeling like a weight pressing down upon her. She clenched her jaw, staring at the dark screen as if it held the key to their case. With a frustrated sigh, she pocketed the device and gazed out of the window, the city lights flickering like distant stars.

"Fine," she muttered under her breath, her voice a mix of irritation and determination. "I'll do this alone."

She couldn't shake the nagging feeling that Ethan Snider was the missing link they had been searching for, the one connection between the victims that no one else had uncovered.

CHAPTER TWENTY FOUR

Olivia turned the key in her door, her weary bones sighing with relief. She had spent another long day at the bar, tending to patrons and their seemingly insatiable thirst for both alcohol and conversation. She managed to keep her exhaustion at bay, offering a warm smile to her neighbors who were out walking their dog late at night.

"Evening, Mr. and Mrs. Johnson," she greeted them, pushing a strand of dark hair behind her ear.

"Hello, Olivia!" Mrs. Johnson replied cheerfully. "How was work today?"

"Same as always," Olivia chuckled. "Busy, but it keeps me on my toes."

As she stepped inside her new home, the faint aroma of lavender welcomed her. The small house wasn't much, but it was hers—a haven for her and her son, Michael, away from the tumultuous past that still haunted her dreams.

Olivia allowed herself a moment to take in the cozy living room, filled with secondhand furniture and photos of happier times. It was a far cry from the luxury she had once known, but it was a price she gladly paid for freedom and safety.

She kicked off her shoes and made her way to the kitchen, pausing to glance at the calendar pinned to the wall. A red circle marked today's date, reminding her that her son was staying over at his friend's house tonight. The thought brought a mixture of emotions—worry, relief, and a pang of loneliness.

With a deep breath, Olivia decided to make the most of her rare free evening. She poured herself a glass of red wine and sank into the plush cushions of her sofa, allowing the stress of the day to melt away. As Olivia sat there, lost in her thoughts, she made a silent promise to herself and her son. No matter what life threw at them, they would face it head-on. They would build a new life—one free from fear, and filled with love and hope.

And for the first time in a long while, that life seemed within reach.

The soft glow of the television cast flickering shadows across the living room, providing a comforting background noise as Olivia continued to unwind. The glass of wine rested on the coffee table, its contents nearly gone, leaving behind a rich, earthy aroma that filled the air. Lost in her thoughts, she absently traced the rim of the glass with her index finger, feeling the smooth, cool surface beneath her touch.

A sudden knock at the door shattered the tranquility of the scene, causing Olivia to jump in surprise. Her heart raced in her chest as she glanced towards the door, wondering who could be visiting so late. Swallowing her unease, she cautiously approached the door and peered through the peephole.

"Good evening," the man greeted her with a smile that didn't quite reach his eyes. He held up a flyer in one hand, and his other hand was tucked into the pocket of his suit jacket. "I'm from a local real estate firm. I just wanted to check in and see how you're liking your new home."

Olivia frowned, her instincts immediately on high alert. "It's after ten p.m.," she said, trying to keep her voice steady. "Why are you visiting so late?"

His smile widened, but it did little to alleviate the sense of unease that settled over her. "Oh, it's just a routine route. I've visited many people tonight; you're not the only one."

Despite her misgivings, Olivia opened the door slightly wider and accepted the flyer he offered her. "Thanks," she murmured, glancing down at the glossy paper.

"Would you like me to go over some new home listings with you?" he asked, attempting to peer past her into the house.

"No, thank you," Olivia replied quickly, firmly shutting thc door and locking it with a decisive click. She leaned against the door for a moment, her heart still pounding against her ribcage. That guy had been way too weird, but she had locked the door now; she was safe.

Letting out a breath, Olivia decided not to let this ruin her night. He was probably being honest and was just a bit strange. Who was she to judge people?

As she moved towards the kitchen, she paused, certain she had heard something click behind her… almost like a lock.

CHAPTER TWENTY FIVE

Morgan found herself standing in front of a rundown building, the last known residence of Ethan Snider. The moonlight cast an eerie glow on the crumbling facade, shadows dancing on the cracked walls as if whispering dark secrets. Her heart thundered in her chest, a sense of foreboding creeping up her spine.

Her phone buzzed in her pocket, causing her to jump. She glanced at the illuminated screen – Derik. She answered, keeping her voice low, "Derik, I'm at the suspect's house."

"Wait for me," he said quickly, the concern evident in his voice. "I was stuck in a damn meeting, that's why I missed your calls."

"I can't wait, Derik. I have to move on this now."

"Dammit, Morgan!" His frustration seeped through the line, but she knew it was rooted in worry. "At least let me—"

She cut him off, hanging up the call. Time was of the essence, and she couldn't afford any delays.

For all she knew, Ethan could be stalking his next victim right now.

Or he could be in this house, planning his next attack.

Either way, this old house was the key. Morgan knew it.

As she approached the decrepit building, Morgan contemplated her life choices. It wasn't too long ago when she was behind bars, framed for a murder she didn't commit. Ten years of hell surrounded by tattooed killers, each inked mark on her body a reminder of who she had become – hardened, fierce, and determined.

But deep down, underneath the tattoos and the tough exterior, she was still driven by a strong sense of justice. That hadn't changed, even after everything she'd been through. And now, she had the chance to prevent another innocent life from being taken.

"Alright, Ethan," she whispered as she stood in front of the crumbling structure, steeling herself for what lay ahead. "It's just you and me now."

The door loomed before Morgan like a specter, hanging open with an eerie invitation. With her heart pounding in her chest, she hesitated for just a moment – the weight of the situation pressing down on her.

Then, gathering her resolve, she stepped inside.

The interior was dimly lit, and she could barely make out the outlines of the room. Each rustle of leaves outside, each creak of the wooden floor beneath her feet sent shivers down her spine. She silently cursed herself for leaving her flashlight in the car but knew there was no time to go back for it. Instead, she relied on her keen instincts to guide her through the darkness.

As she cautiously explored Ethan's lair, her eyes slowly adjusted to the gloom. Her surroundings revealed themselves in fragments: A worn sofa, a rickety table cluttered with papers, and a damp, musty scent hanging in the air. But it was when she stumbled upon a hidden room that her blood truly ran cold.

"Jesus Christ," she muttered, taking in the horrifying display before her.

Lock-picking tools gleamed in the faint light, and blueprints of victims' homes were strewn across the floor as if they were confetti at some twisted celebration. Morgan's hands shook as she picked up one of the papers.

"Olivia," she breathed, her eyes locked onto the name written at the top of the blueprint. The realization hit her like a punch to the gut – Ethan was planning his next kill, and she had to stop him before it was too late.

She sprinted out of the house, leaving Ethan's lair behind her. But even as she raced toward her car, a nagging fear gnawed at the edges of her mind – would she be too late to save Olivia?

***

The tires of Morgan's car screeched in protest as she tore through the darkened streets of Charlesberg, her heart thundering in her chest. The radio crackled with static, and Derik's voice broke through the noise.

"Did you send me the address?" he asked urgently, his words slightly slurred from exhaustion.

"Check your messages!" Morgan snapped, gripping the steering wheel with white-knuckled intensity. "I think Ethan's there now. He's going to kill Olivia if we don't hurry."

"Wait for backup, Morgan," Derik pleaded, the desperation in his voice a mirror of Morgan's own mounting fear. "We'll get there faster if we work together."

"Can't afford to wait," she replied tersely, her dark hair whipping around her face as she accelerated even further. The ink on her arms seemed to writhe like serpents in the dim glow of the dashboard lights.

"Damn it, Morgan, I know you want to protect her," Derik said, his voice strained. "But you can't just risk your life by rushing in without a plan."

"Olivia doesn't have time for a plan, Derik," Morgan shot back, her voice thick with emotion. She could almost see the green fire in his eyes, burning with determination and remorse for his past actions. But she had already forgiven him, and now they needed to act.

"Please, just wait for me," Derik begged one last time, his voice cracking under the weight of his concern.

"Sorry, Derik," was all Morgan could muster before hanging up and tossing her phone onto the passenger seat. She knew that she was defying protocol, but the thought of another life being snuffed out at Ethan's hands was too much to bear.

As the houses blurred past her, Morgan thought of Olivia, whoever she was, and hoped beyond hope that she would arrive in time. The cold feeling in her gut grew heavier with each passing second, yet she pressed on, her resolve unwavering.

"Please," she whispered into the night, her breath fogging up the windshield. "Let me get there in time."

CHAPTER TWENTY SIX

The tires screeched as Morgan's car came to an abrupt halt outside Olivia's house. The quiet suburban street seemed deceptively serene, its tranquility marred only by the distant hum of traffic and the occasional rustle of leaves in the night breeze. She unholstered her gun, gripping the handle so tightly that the knuckles on her hand turned white.

Her heart pounded like a sledgehammer against her ribcage. As a seasoned agent, she was no stranger to fear—but the thought of losing another innocent life sent ice coursing through her veins, mingling with the fire that burned for justice.

Morgan approached the house with careful, measured steps, keeping to the shadows cast by the dim glow of the streetlights. Her eyes darted from one corner to another, scanning the surroundings for any sign of movement or danger. Every step closer to the door felt like wading through treacle; time stretched cruelly slow, taunting her efforts.

"Come on, come on," she whispered to herself, trying to quell the rising tide of desperation within her. A decade's worth of regrets weighed heavily upon her shoulders, each unsolved case and lost life etching a new line of sorrow onto her soul. Tonight, she refused to let that list grow any longer.

Crouching beneath a window, Morgan cautiously peered inside. There, in the warm glow of the kitchen light, stood Olivia—alive. Relief washed over her, but only for a fleeting moment. Her breath caught in her throat as she spied Ethan, creeping through the shadows, clutching a rock in his hand.

He was going to bludgeon Olivia to death if Morgan didn't act fast.

With a surge of adrenaline, Morgan made her decision. She pulled back her leg and kicked the door in, sending splinters flying as it slammed open. Olivia screamed, startled by the sudden intrusion, while Ethan turned to face Morgan with a mixture of horror and rage.

"Stop right there!" Morgan barked, lunging forward. "FBI!"

But Ethan was quick to react. With a guttural snarl, he charged at Morgan, brandishing the rock like a weapon. Instincts honed from years of experience took over, and she sidestepped his attack, delivering a sharp elbow to his ribs. The impact sent him staggering but didn't deter him for long.

"Olivia, run!" Morgan shouted, her attention fixed on the threat before her. She could hear the panicked sobs of the woman behind her and knew that every second counted in preventing another victim from succumbing to Ethan's twisted desires.

Chaos erupted in the small living room as Morgan grappled with Ethan. Their struggle was raw and unrelenting, neither willing to give an inch. A coffee table toppled, shattering a vase and scattering its contents across the floor. Pictures fell from their hooks, glass crunching beneath their feet as they fought.

"Get off me!" Ethan growled, his breath hot against Morgan's face as they wrestled for control. His grip tightened around the rock, his knuckles turning white from the strain.

Morgan gritted her teeth, refusing to let fear or pain dictate her actions. She couldn't afford to lose this fight—not when Olivia's life hung in the balance.

"Think you can just waltz in here and ruin my plans?" Ethan spat, his voice dripping with venom. "You're going to regret laying a hand on me."

"Your sick games end tonight," Morgan retorted, her icy gaze never wavering from his twisted features. She knew she couldn't afford to let his words get under her skin, not when the stakes were so high.

With a roar of frustration, Ethan lunged again, and Morgan met his attack with calculated precision. She blocked his strike, redirecting his momentum to send him stumbling off-balance. As he tried to recover, she pressed her advantage, landing a powerful blow that sent him crashing into the wall.

"Stay down," she commanded, her chest heaving with exertion. But as she looked around the room, taking in the shattered remnants of Olivia's life, she knew that their fight was far from over.

The cacophony of destruction echoed through the once tranquil suburb like a thunderclap, shattering the peaceful night air. Morgan's heart pounded in her ears as she grappled with Ethan, each desperate to gain the upper hand.

"Olivia, run!" Morgan shouted between clenched teeth, her breath ragged from exertion. She managed to pin one of Ethan's arms behind his back, but it was like trying to contain a wild animal. "Find somewhere safe and stay there!"

Olivia hesitated, her eyes wide with terror as she took in the scene before her – the woman who'd burst into her home locked in a deadly struggle with the man who'd been hiding in the shadows. But Morgan's words seemed to break through her shock, and Olivia stumbled toward the hallway, disappearing from sight.

Amid the chaos, Morgan spared a brief thought for Derik. Despite her urgent pleas for backup, she knew he was still minutes away at best. She couldn't rely on anyone but herself right now. The responsibility weighed heavy on her shoulders, but she gritted her teeth and pushed the thought aside, focusing instead on the man who threatened to tear them all apart.

"Give up, Ethan!" she snarled, twisting his arm further. "You're not going to win this."

"Go to hell," Ethan spat, his face contorted in pain and fury. He lunged forward, catching Morgan off-guard and managing to free his arm. With renewed desperation, he swung the rock towards her head.

Morgan ducked just in time, feeling the rush of air as the rock narrowly missed her temple. Her adrenaline surged, fueling her every action as she countered Ethan's attack with a swift kick to his midsection.

"Damn you!" Ethan roared, doubling over from the impact. But even as he staggered back, his eyes were filled with a chilling determination that made Morgan's spine crawl.

"Derik," Morgan whispered under her breath, praying for her partner to arrive before it was too late. She couldn't afford to lose this battle – not with Olivia's life hanging in the balance.

As if sensing her thoughts, Ethan let out a sinister chuckle. "You think you can save her?" he taunted, his voice dripping with malice. "You're just delaying the inevitable."

"Shut up!" Morgan gritted out, lunging forward once more, her movements driven by sheer desperation. She couldn't – wouldn't – let him hurt Olivia. She had to end this now.

Summoning every ounce of strength she possessed, Morgan's muscles tensed as she prepared to make her final move. She lunged forward, catching Ethan off-guard, and wrestled the rock from his grasp. With a quick twist of her wrist, she wrenched his arm behind him and slammed him face-first onto the ground.

"Stay down!" she snarled through gritted teeth, her heart pounding in her ears. The metallic click of handcuffs echoed in the room as she secured Ethan's wrists together, ensuring that he couldn't cause any more harm.

"Olivia," Morgan called out, her voice breathless but firm. "It's okay. You're safe now."

From her hiding spot behind an overturned table, Olivia peeked out, her eyes widening with relief when she saw Ethan restrained on the floor. "Thank you," she whispered, tears streaming down her cheeks.

"Everything's going to be alright," Morgan reassured her, though she knew that the scars left by this night would take time to heal.

As if on cue, the distant wail of sirens grew louder, the sound both comforting and unnerving. Relief washed over Morgan, and she allowed herself a brief moment to close her eyes and steady her breathing before returning her focus to the situation at hand.

"Backup's here," she informed Olivia, rising to her feet and maintaining a watchful eye on Ethan. He glared up at her, his eyes burning with hatred, but she refused to let him rattle her.

The front door burst open, and a flood of law enforcement officers swarmed into the house, securing the scene with swift precision. Among them was Derik, his green eyes wide with a mixture of concern and relief as they locked onto Morgan.

"Jesus, Morgan," he breathed, rushing to her side. "Are you okay?"

"Yeah," she replied, nodding toward the handcuffed Ethan. "We got him."

Derik's gaze flicked over to Olivia, who was now wrapped in a comforting blanket as she spoke with another officer. "And the victim?"

"Safe," Morgan confirmed, feeling a wave of pride for having successfully protected her. "It's finally over, Derik. We caught the killer."

"Thanks to you," he said, his voice filled with admiration. The weight of the world seemed to lift from his shoulders as he exhaled deeply. "I don't know what we would have done without you."

"Let's just make sure this never happens again," Morgan replied, her thoughts drifting to the victims who had suffered at Ethan's hands. She knew that there would always be darkness in the world, but tonight, at least, they had managed to bring one monster to justice.

EPILOGUE

Morgan stumbled into her house late at night, fatigue etching lines on her face. The silence of the darkened living room was deafening, far from the loving welcome she once knew. She tossed her keys onto the console table, the metallic clatter echoing like the sound of chains in the emptiness.

"Damn you, Thomas," she whispered, cursing the handsome agent who had taken more than just her trust.

Her loyal Pitbull, Skunk, was gone—kidnapped by the very man who had pretended to care for her. Morgan's heart ached at the thought of her missing companion, and she couldn't shake the feeling of cold abandonment that filled her home.

She allowed herself a moment to think about the case she'd just closed. Ethan Snider, the sick bastard who had preyed on innocent women, would finally be going to trial. His victims would have justice, and he'd spend the rest of his life rotting behind bars.

But despite their success, a hollow emptiness gnawed at her insides, leaving her with the bitter taste of ash on her tongue. She clasped her hands together, trying to suppress the tremors that threatened to overtake her.

None of this brings Skunk back, or fixes what happened ten years ago, she thought bitterly, her voice cracking under the weight of the memories that haunted her every waking moment.

Morgan knew she should be grateful for the victories they achieved, yet it wasn't enough. That somehow, she was still paying for sins she didn't even know she had committed.

Taking a deep breath, Morgan moved toward the couch, her eyes heavy with fatigue. As she was about to sit down, the sight of scattered files on the coffee table stopped her in her tracks. Her heart raced as her muscles tensed; Thomas had broken into her house again. The last time he'd done this, he'd left Skunk's collar as a chilling warning.

"Dammit, Thomas," she hissed under her breath, fury simmering beneath the surface.

Her hands shook as she reached for the files, careful not to disturb any potential evidence. Flipping them open, she found they were from an old FBI case, marked with bold REDACTED labels and CONFIDENTIAL stamps. Her mouth went dry, the bitter taste of ash still lingering on her tongue from earlier thoughts.

In that moment, she saw it—an unexpected face staring back at her. It was her father, young and dapper in a suit, looking every bit the part of an FBI agent. The name next to his picture read "John Christopher" instead of the familiar "Christopher Cross" she had always known him by.

"John Christopher?" she whispered, her voice wavering as she traced her fingers over the photograph. "Why would you hide this?"

Morgan's mind raced as she tried to make sense of the revelation, her heart pounding in her chest. She felt betrayed by both her father and Thomas, who seemed to be toying with her like a puppet on strings.

"Was this your secret, Dad?" she wondered aloud, her voice barely above a whisper. "Is this why I've been targeted all these years? What am I missing?"

She continued to dig deeper into the file, her resolve growing stronger with each new piece of information she uncovered. Whatever connection her father had to the FBI, and to John Christopher, she was determined to uncover it. And when she did, Thomas Grady would finally pay for the pain he'd brought into her life.

Morgan's fingers shook as she flipped through the pages, her heartbeat drumming in her ears. Each new piece of information felt like a punch to the gut, but she couldn't stop herself from devouring every word. The truth about her father, hidden for so long, was finally laid bare before her.

"Christopher Cross" had been nothing more than a carefully crafted alias. He'd changed his name and identity to protect both himself and those around him. But why? What could possibly have driven him to such extremes?

As she dug deeper into the file, Morgan found her answer. A heavily redacted section spoke of an operation gone wrong – a woman caught in the cross-fire, her life snuffed out by an errant bullet. And the agent responsible: John Christopher, her father.

Morgan's hands trembled as she held the file, the words swimming before her eyes. "You killed someone, Dad," she whispered, feeling as though someone had ripped the ground from beneath her feet. She leaned back against the couch for support, her chest tightening with each ragged breath.

Thomas isn't after me because of what I did, she realized, the pieces of the puzzle falling into place. *He's after me because of you.*

The person who framed me… it was all because of you.

Thomas is probably just his puppet, but all of this… is because of you, Dad.

Her heart ached. Her thoughts raced as she considered the implications. Her father had been haunted by his past, and now that same darkness threatened to consume her. Someone in the FBI had framed her for murder, made her suffer for her father's sins, and she would never be free until she brought him to justice.

She wasn't sure who the real man who had framed her was—maybe it was Thomas, but she doubted it. She was certain Thomas was just a pawn, having too much fun with Morgan, sent on behalf of the man—or men—who had framed her. The same people who'd attempted to blackmail Derik into betraying her.

She had to find out who they were, but first thing was first—she had to deal with Thomas Grady.

She looked at the files scattered across the table, their presence a testament to Thomas's relentless pursuit. If he'd broken into her home once again, it meant he was still watching her, waiting for her to crack.

"Fine," she whispered, her voice barely audible. "You want a fight? You've got one."

With renewed determination, Morgan closed the file and stood up. Thomas Grady had taken everything from her – her father's secret past, her dog, her freedom. But he would not take her spirit. She would uncover the truth, expose his crimes, and make him pay for what he'd done.

NOW AVAILABLE!

FORLORN
(A Morgan Cross FBI Suspense Thriller—Book Ten)

When macabre murder scenes depict occult legends across the city's landmarks, only ex-con FBI Agent Morgan Cross can decipher the signs etched by a diabolical killer—and stop him before it's too late.

"A masterpiece of thriller and mystery."
—Books and Movie Reviews, Roberto Mattos (re Once Gone)

FORLORN is book #10 in a long-anticipated new series by #1 bestseller and USA Today bestselling author Blake Pierce, whose bestseller Once Gone (a free download) has received over 7,000 five star ratings and reviews.

Superstar FBI Agent Morgan Cross was at the height of her career when she was framed, wrongly imprisoned, and sent to do 10 hard years in prison. Finally exonerated and set free, Morgan emerges from jail as a changed person—hardened, ruthless, closed off to the world, and unsure how to start again.

When the FBI comes knocking, desperately needing Morgan to return and hunt down a killer who seems to be obsessed with drowning, Morgan is torn.

Morgan is not the same person, no longer willing to play by the rules, and will stop at nothing this time.

In a non-stop thriller, it will be a deadly cat and mouse chase between a diabolical killer and an ex-con FBI agent who has nothing left to lose—with a new victim's fate riding on it all.

A page-turning and harrowing crime thriller featuring a brilliant and tortured FBI agent, the Morgan Cross series is a riveting mystery, packed with non-stop action, suspense, twists and turns, revelations, and driven by a breakneck pace that will keep you flipping pages late into the night. Fans of Rachel Caine, Teresa Driscoll and Robert Dugoni are sure to fall in love.

Future books in the series will be available soon!

"An edge of your seat thriller in a new series that keeps you turning pages! ...So many twists, turns and red herrings… I can't wait to see what happens next."
—Reader review (Her Last Wish)

"A strong, complex story about two FBI agents trying to stop a serial killer. If you want an author to capture your attention and have you guessing, yet trying to put the pieces together, Pierce is your author!"
—Reader review (Her Last Wish)

"A typical Blake Pierce twisting, turning, roller coaster ride suspense thriller. Will have you turning the pages to the last sentence of the last chapter!!!"
—Reader review (City of Prey)

"Right from the start we have an unusual protagonist that I haven't seen done in this genre before. The action is nonstop… A very atmospheric novel that will keep you turning pages well into the wee hours."
—Reader review (City of Prey)

"Everything that I look for in a book… a great plot, interesting characters, and grabs your interest right away. The book moves along at a breakneck pace and stays that way until the end. Now on go I to book two!"
—Reader review (Girl, Alone)

"Exciting, heart pounding, edge of your seat book… a must read for mystery and suspense readers!"
—Reader review (Girl, Alone)

Blake Pierce

Blake Pierce is the USA Today bestselling author of the RILEY PAGE mystery series, which includes seventeen books. Blake Pierce is also the author of the MACKENZIE WHITE mystery series, comprising fourteen books; of the AVERY BLACK mystery series, comprising six books; of the KERI LOCKE mystery series, comprising five books; of the MAKING OF RILEY PAIGE mystery series, comprising six books; of the KATE WISE mystery series, comprising seven books; of the CHLOE FINE psychological suspense mystery, comprising six books; of the JESSIE HUNT psychological suspense thriller series, comprising thirty-five books (and counting); of the AU PAIR psychological suspense thriller series, comprising three books; of the ZOE PRIME mystery series, comprising six books; of the ADELE SHARP mystery series, comprising sixteen books, of the EUROPEAN VOYAGE cozy mystery series, comprising six books; of the LAURA FROST FBI suspense thriller, comprising eleven books; of the ELLA DARK FBI suspense thriller, comprising twenty-one books (and counting); of the A YEAR IN EUROPE cozy mystery series, comprising nine books, of the AVA GOLD mystery series, comprising six books; of the RACHEL GIFT mystery series, comprising fifteen books (and counting); of the VALERIE LAW mystery series, comprising nine books; of the PAIGE KING mystery series, comprising eight books; of the MAY MOORE mystery series, comprising eleven books; of the CORA SHIELDS mystery series, comprising eight books; of the NICKY LYONS mystery series, comprising eight books, of the CAMI LARK mystery series, comprising ten books; of the AMBER YOUNG mystery series, comprising seven books (and counting); of the DAISY FORTUNE mystery series, comprising five books; of the FIONA RED mystery series, comprising eleven books (and counting); of the FAITH BOLD mystery series, comprising fourteen books (and counting); of the JULIETTE HART mystery series, comprising five books (and counting); of the MORGAN CROSS mystery series, comprising ten books (and counting); of the FINN WRIGHT mystery series, comprising six books (and counting); of the new SHEILA STONE suspense thriller series, comprising five books (and counting); and of the new RACHEL BLACKWOOD suspense thriller series, comprising five books (and counting).

An avid reader and lifelong fan of the mystery and thriller genres, Blake loves to hear from you, so please feel free to visit www.blakepierceauthor.com to learn more and stay in touch.

BOOKS BY BLAKE PIERCE

RACHEL BLACKWOOD SUSPENSE THRILLER
NOT THIS WAY (Book #1)
NOT THIS TIME (Book #2)
NOT THIS CLOSE (Book #3)
NOT THIS ROAD (Book #4)
NOT THIS LATE (Book #5)

SHEILA STONE SUSPENSE THRILLER
SILENT GIRL (Book #1)
SILENT TRAIL (Book #2)
SILENT NIGHT (Book #3)
SILENT HOUSE (Book #4)
SILENT SCREAM (Book #5)

FINN WRIGHT MYSTERY SERIES
WHEN YOU'RE MINE (Book #1)
WHEN YOU'RE SAFE (Book #2)
WHEN YOU'RE CLOSE (Book #3)
WHEN YOU'RE SLEEPING (Book #4)
WHEN YOU'RE SANE (Book #5)
WHEN YOU'RE SILENT (Book #6)

MORGAN CROSS MYSTERY SERIES
FOR YOU (Book #1)
FOR RAGE (Book #2)
FOR LUST (Book #3)
FOR WRATH (Book #4)
FOREVER (Book #5)
FOR US (Book #6)
FOR NOW (Book #7)
FOR ONCE (Book #8)
FOR ETERNITY (Book #9)
FORLORN (Book #10)

JULIETTE HART MYSTERY SERIES
NOTHING TO FEAR (Book #1)
NOTHING THERE (Book #2)
NOTHING WATCHING (Book #3)
NOTHING HIDING (Book #4)
NOTHING LEFT (Book #5)

FAITH BOLD MYSTERY SERIES
SO LONG (Book #1)
SO COLD (Book #2)
SO SCARED (Book #3)
SO NORMAL (Book #4)
SO FAR GONE (Book #5)
SO LOST (Book #6)
SO ALONE (Book #7)
SO FORGOTTEN (Book #8)
SO INSANE (Book #9)
SO SMITTEN (Book #10)
SO SIMPLE (Book #11)
SO BROKEN (Book #12)
SO CRUEL (Book #13)
SO HAUNTED (Book #14)

FIONA RED MYSTERY SERIES
LET HER GO (Book #1)
LET HER BE (Book #2)
LET HER HOPE (Book #3)
LET HER WISH (Book #4)
LET HER LIVE (Book #5)
LET HER RUN (Book #6)
LET HER HIDE (Book #7)
LET HER BELIEVE (Book #8)
LET HER FORGET (Book #9)
LET HER TRY (Book #10)
LET HER PLAY (Book #11)

DAISY FORTUNE MYSTERY SERIES
NEED YOU (Book #1)
CLAIM YOU (Book #2)
CRAVE YOU (Book #3)

CHOOSE YOU (Book #4)
CHASE YOU (Book #5)

AMBER YOUNG MYSTERY SERIES
ABSENT PITY (Book #1)
ABSENT REMORSE (Book #2)
ABSENT FEELING (Book #3)
ABSENT MERCY (Book #4)
ABSENT REASON (Book #5)
ABSENT SANITY (Book #6)
ABSENT LIFE (Book #7)

CAMI LARK MYSTERY SERIES
JUST ME (Book #1)
JUST OUTSIDE (Book #2)
JUST RIGHT (Book #3)
JUST FORGET (Book #4)
JUST ONCE (Book #5)
JUST HIDE (Book #6)
JUST NOW (Book #7)
JUST HOPE (Book #8)
JUST LEAVE (Book #9)
JUST TONIGHT (Book #10)

NICKY LYONS MYSTERY SERIES
ALL MINE (Book #1)
ALL HIS (Book #2)
ALL HE SEES (Book #3)
ALL ALONE (Book #4)
ALL FOR ONE (Book #5)
ALL HE TAKES (Book #6)
ALL FOR ME (Book #7)
ALL IN (Book #8)

CORA SHIELDS MYSTERY SERIES
UNDONE (Book #1)
UNWANTED (Book #2)
UNHINGED (Book #3)
UNSAID (Book #4)
UNGLUED (Book #5)

UNSTABLE (Book #6)
UNKNOWN (Book #7)
UNAWARE (Book #8)

MAY MOORE SUSPENSE THRILLER
NEVER RUN (Book #1)
NEVER TELL (Book #2)
NEVER LIVE (Book #3)
NEVER HIDE (Book #4)
NEVER FORGIVE (Book #5)
NEVER AGAIN (Book #6)
NEVER LOOK BACK (Book #7)
NEVER FORGET (Book #8)
NEVER LET GO (Book #9)
NEVER PRETEND (Book #10)
NEVER HESITATE (Book #11)

PAIGE KING MYSTERY SERIES
THE GIRL HE PINED (Book #1)
THE GIRL HE CHOSE (Book #2)
THE GIRL HE TOOK (Book #3)
THE GIRL HE WISHED (Book #4)
THE GIRL HE CROWNED (Book #5)
THE GIRL HE WATCHED (Book #6)
THE GIRL HE WANTED (Book #7)
THE GIRL HE CLAIMED (Book #8)

VALERIE LAW MYSTERY SERIES
NO MERCY (Book #1)
NO PITY (Book #2)
NO FEAR (Book #3)
NO SLEEP (Book #4)
NO QUARTER (Book #5)
NO CHANCE (Book #6)
NO REFUGE (Book #7)
NO GRACE (Book #8)
NO ESCAPE (Book #9)

RACHEL GIFT MYSTERY SERIES
HER LAST WISH (Book #1)

HER LAST CHANCE (Book #2)
HER LAST HOPE (Book #3)
HER LAST FEAR (Book #4)
HER LAST CHOICE (Book #5)
HER LAST BREATH (Book #6)
HER LAST MISTAKE (Book #7)
HER LAST DESIRE (Book #8)
HER LAST REGRET (Book #9)
HER LAST HOUR (Book #10)
HER LAST SHOT (Book #11)
HER LAST PRAYER (Book #12)
HER LAST LIE (Book #13)
HER LAST WHISPER (Book #14)
HER LAST SECRET (Book #15)

AVA GOLD MYSTERY SERIES
CITY OF PREY (Book #1)
CITY OF FEAR (Book #2)
CITY OF BONES (Book #3)
CITY OF GHOSTS (Book #4)
CITY OF DEATH (Book #5)
CITY OF VICE (Book #6)

A YEAR IN EUROPE
A MURDER IN PARIS (Book #1)
DEATH IN FLORENCE (Book #2)
VENGEANCE IN VIENNA (Book #3)
A FATALITY IN SPAIN (Book #4)

ELLA DARK FBI SUSPENSE THRILLER
GIRL, ALONE (Book #1)
GIRL, TAKEN (Book #2)
GIRL, HUNTED (Book #3)
GIRL, SILENCED (Book #4)
GIRL, VANISHED (Book 5)
GIRL ERASED (Book #6)
GIRL, FORSAKEN (Book #7)
GIRL, TRAPPED (Book #8)
GIRL, EXPENDABLE (Book #9)
GIRL, ESCAPED (Book #10)

GIRL, HIS (Book #11)
GIRL, LURED (Book #12)
GIRL, MISSING (Book #13)
GIRL, UNKNOWN (Book #14)
GIRL, DECEIVED (Book #15)
GIRL, FORLORN (Book #16)
GIRL, REMADE (Book #17)
GIRL, BETRAYED (Book #18)
GIRL, BOUND (Book #19)
GIRL, REFORMED (Book #20)
GIRL, REBORN (Book #21)

LAURA FROST FBI SUSPENSE THRILLER
ALREADY GONE (Book #1)
ALREADY SEEN (Book #2)
ALREADY TRAPPED (Book #3)
ALREADY MISSING (Book #4)
ALREADY DEAD (Book #5)
ALREADY TAKEN (Book #6)
ALREADY CHOSEN (Book #7)
ALREADY LOST (Book #8)
ALREADY HIS (Book #9)
ALREADY LURED (Book #10)
ALREADY COLD (Book #11)

EUROPEAN VOYAGE COZY MYSTERY SERIES
MURDER (AND BAKLAVA) (Book #1)
DEATH (AND APPLE STRUDEL) (Book #2)
CRIME (AND LAGER) (Book #3)
MISFORTUNE (AND GOUDA) (Book #4)
CALAMITY (AND A DANISH) (Book #5)
MAYHEM (AND HERRING) (Book #6)

ADELE SHARP MYSTERY SERIES
LEFT TO DIE (Book #1)
LEFT TO RUN (Book #2)
LEFT TO HIDE (Book #3)
LEFT TO KILL (Book #4)
LEFT TO MURDER (Book #5)
LEFT TO ENVY (Book #6)

LEFT TO LAPSE (Book #7)
LEFT TO VANISH (Book #8)
LEFT TO HUNT (Book #9)
LEFT TO FEAR (Book #10)
LEFT TO PREY (Book #11)
LEFT TO LURE (Book #12)
LEFT TO CRAVE (Book #13)
LEFT TO LOATHE (Book #14)
LEFT TO HARM (Book #15)
LEFT TO RUIN (Book #16)

THE AU PAIR SERIES
ALMOST GONE (Book#1)
ALMOST LOST (Book #2)
ALMOST DEAD (Book #3)

ZOE PRIME MYSTERY SERIES
FACE OF DEATH (Book#1)
FACE OF MURDER (Book #2)
FACE OF FEAR (Book #3)
FACE OF MADNESS (Book #4)
FACE OF FURY (Book #5)
FACE OF DARKNESS (Book #6)

A JESSIE HUNT PSYCHOLOGICAL SUSPENSE SERIES
THE PERFECT WIFE (Book #1)
THE PERFECT BLOCK (Book #2)
THE PERFECT HOUSE (Book #3)
THE PERFECT SMILE (Book #4)
THE PERFECT LIE (Book #5)
THE PERFECT LOOK (Book #6)
THE PERFECT AFFAIR (Book #7)
THE PERFECT ALIBI (Book #8)
THE PERFECT NEIGHBOR (Book #9)
THE PERFECT DISGUISE (Book #10)
THE PERFECT SECRET (Book #11)
THE PERFECT FAÇADE (Book #12)
THE PERFECT IMPRESSION (Book #13)
THE PERFECT DECEIT (Book #14)
THE PERFECT MISTRESS (Book #15)

THE PERFECT IMAGE (Book #16)
THE PERFECT VEIL (Book #17)
THE PERFECT INDISCRETION (Book #18)
THE PERFECT RUMOR (Book #19)
THE PERFECT COUPLE (Book #20)
THE PERFECT MURDER (Book #21)
THE PERFECT HUSBAND (Book #22)
THE PERFECT SCANDAL (Book #23)
THE PERFECT MASK (Book #24)
THE PERFECT RUSE (Book #25)
THE PERFECT VENEER (Book #26)
THE PERFECT PEOPLE (Book #27)
THE PERFECT WITNESS (Book #28)
THE PERFECT APPEARANCE (Book #29)
THE PERFECT TRAP (Book #30)
THE PERFECT EXPRESSION (Book #31)
THE PERFECT ACCOMPLICE (Book #32)
THE PERFECT SHOW (Book #33)
THE PERFECT POISE (Book #34)
THE PERFECT CROWD (Book #35)

CHLOE FINE PSYCHOLOGICAL SUSPENSE SERIES
NEXT DOOR (Book #1)
A NEIGHBOR'S LIE (Book #2)
CUL DE SAC (Book #3)
SILENT NEIGHBOR (Book #4)
HOMECOMING (Book #5)
TINTED WINDOWS (Book #6)

KATE WISE MYSTERY SERIES
IF SHE KNEW (Book #1)
IF SHE SAW (Book #2)
IF SHE RAN (Book #3)
IF SHE HID (Book #4)
IF SHE FLED (Book #5)
IF SHE FEARED (Book #6)
IF SHE HEARD (Book #7)

THE MAKING OF RILEY PAIGE SERIES
WATCHING (Book #1)

WAITING (Book #2)
LURING (Book #3)
TAKING (Book #4)
STALKING (Book #5)
KILLING (Book #6)

RILEY PAIGE MYSTERY SERIES
ONCE GONE (Book #1)
ONCE TAKEN (Book #2)
ONCE CRAVED (Book #3)
ONCE LURED (Book #4)
ONCE HUNTED (Book #5)
ONCE PINED (Book #6)
ONCE FORSAKEN (Book #7)
ONCE COLD (Book #8)
ONCE STALKED (Book #9)
ONCE LOST (Book #10)
ONCE BURIED (Book #11)
ONCE BOUND (Book #12)
ONCE TRAPPED (Book #13)
ONCE DORMANT (Book #14)
ONCE SHUNNED (Book #15)
ONCE MISSED (Book #16)
ONCE CHOSEN (Book #17)

MACKENZIE WHITE MYSTERY SERIES
BEFORE HE KILLS (Book #1)
BEFORE HE SEES (Book #2)
BEFORE HE COVETS (Book #3)
BEFORE HE TAKES (Book #4)
BEFORE HE NEEDS (Book #5)
BEFORE HE FEELS (Book #6)
BEFORE HE SINS (Book #7)
BEFORE HE HUNTS (Book #8)
BEFORE HE PREYS (Book #9)
BEFORE HE LONGS (Book #10)
BEFORE HE LAPSES (Book #11)
BEFORE HE ENVIES (Book #12)
BEFORE HE STALKS (Book #13)
BEFORE HE HARMS (Book #14)

AVERY BLACK MYSTERY SERIES
CAUSE TO KILL (Book #1)
CAUSE TO RUN (Book #2)
CAUSE TO HIDE (Book #3)
CAUSE TO FEAR (Book #4)
CAUSE TO SAVE (Book #5)
CAUSE TO DREAD (Book #6)

KERI LOCKE MYSTERY SERIES
A TRACE OF DEATH (Book #1)
A TRACE OF MURDER (Book #2)
A TRACE OF VICE (Book #3)
A TRACE OF CRIME (Book #4)
A TRACE OF HOPE (Book #5)

Manufactured by Amazon.ca
Acheson, AB